Bird
in a
Cage

by Anne Schraff

☑ **W9-BON-496**

Perfection Learning® Corporation
Logan, Iowa 51546

Cover Design: Mark Hagenberg

Cover Image Credit: © Images.com/CORBIS

For information, contact:
Perfection Learning® Corporation
1000 North Second Avenue, P.O. Box 500,
Logan, Iowa 51546-0500.
Phone: 1-800-831-4190 • Fax: 1-800-543-2745
perfectionlearning.com

Paperback ISBN 0-7891-6659-3
Reinforced Library Binding ISBN 0-7569-4757-x

1 2 3 4 5 6 PP 09 08 07 06 05

1 CLINT ASUNA WAS hurrying back to his pickup to grab his biology homework when he first saw her. She was crouching in terror beside his truck, her long dark hair disheveled, her eyes wide.

"Shhh," she cried, "Don't give me away!"

"What's the matter?" Clint asked.

"Pretend you don't see me," she whispered. "Oh, please. He's watching!"

Maybe it was a joke. He had wacky friends who sometimes did this kind of thing. The guys at Grissom High School were always up to something. Maybe they hired this strange, beautiful girl just to rattle Clint's cage. Clint glanced around, expecting to see one of the jokers popping into view. His friends Dale McGee and Ricky Wilkins were the most likely culprits. He decided to go along with it.

"Is he still there?" the girl asked.

"Who?" Clint asked, staying cool.

"Don't look at me when you talk to me," the girl pleaded. "The older man. The older fat man in the tweed jacket. Is he still there?"

She continued to kneel on the asphalt beside the truck.

Clint looked around. He didn't see a fat man in a tweed jacket.

"Don't see anybody like that now," Clint said, smiling a little.

This had to be a gag. The girl got up slowly. She looked around and breathed a sigh of relief. "Thanks a lot. Thank you for helping me," she said, reaching out to touch Clint's arm in a gesture of gratitude.

"You're welcome," Clint said, looking down at her slim fingers on his arm. "What's going on? Do you go to school here? I don't think I've seen you around Grissom before."

"I am Melina Barja. I just started here, so I haven't met many people yet," she said. "This is your car?"

"Yeah," Clint answered as he looked more closely at Melina. She was even more beautiful than she first appeared. He had never seen such a lovely girl. "I'm

Clint Asuna. I'm a junior here. So . . . who was the guy in the tweed jacket and what did he want with you?"

"Maybe it was nothing," she said. "I just saw this strange man staring at me and I got frightened. I do not know why he . . . he frightened me. I . . . I did not think. I just hid here."

"Is somebody after you or something?" Clint asked as he got his bag out of his truck. He could see she was very nervous. She had a strong accent, but she seemed to be stumbling over her words more from fright than from unfamiliarity with the language.

"It's all right. I'm okay now," she said. "Could you tell me where the bus stop is?"

"You mean the city bus or the school buses?" Clint asked.

"The school bus, please. My foster mother brought me here today, but I will need the bus to go home," Melina said.

"I can give you a lift home after school if you want." Clint offered. The thought of having this beautiful girl in his pickup was irresistible.

"Oh, that is very kind. I chose well

when I hid here," she said. "I must be lucky—meeting you today. Can you show me the science building? I have a biology class now."

"Biology II? With Ms. Reynosa?" Clint asked. He felt like *he* must be the lucky one. "I'm headed there too, so I can show you."

As they walked to class, Clint tried to place Melina's accent. Maybe Greek or Italian, he thought. Whatever it was, it was exotic and delightful, just like everything else about her.

Clint's friends Dale and Ricky were waiting outside the classroom. They stared at the girl walking by his side. Clint couldn't resist grinning at his buddies. He felt like the first kid on the block to get the coolest new bike. He enjoyed the envy in the eyes of his friends.

As they entered the room, Melina looked at him, "This is your class? I am so glad we are together first thing. It will get the day started right," she said, smiling. Then she walked to the teacher's desk.

Ms. Reynosa sat Melina in an empty seat toward the front, which gave Clint plenty of opportunity to admire Melina during lulls in the lecture. Dale and Ricky looked at Clint then back at Melina.

"Who's that?" Ricky whispered, "How come she's with you?"

Clint just grinned to himself again. He knew he looked okay, but he wasn't the most handsome guy around. Dale was tall with curly red hair and classic features, and Ricky had a magnetic, funny personality. Usually, girls were much more drawn to the two of them than to Clint, who tended to be shy around girls.

After class, Clint waited for Melina to make her way to the door.

"Hi, Clint," Melina said cheerfully.

"Did you like the class, Melina?" Clint asked.

"I am not so good at science. Is the teacher nice?" she asked.

"Ms. Reynosa explains stuff really well," Clint said, "and if you don't understand something, I'll help you too. We can study together."

"Oh, you are so nice," Melina said, moving a little closer to Clint as they walked away from the building. She showed him her schedule and asked the way to her next class. Dale and Ricky followed not too far behind.

As Melina headed off toward the art building, Clint joined his friends. As the boys walked to English class, Dale and Ricky grilled Clint about Melina. Clint just said he'd met her that morning and was only trying to be helpful. He shrugged off their questions, but he knew what they were thinking because he was thinking it too. Melina could be a movie star with those looks and that sly smile. Why did she choose Clint?

As Clint ate his lunch later, he spotted Melina across the cafeteria. She had a sack lunch and was wandering among the tables, looking for a spot to sit. Clint had just decided to call out to her when he saw her sit at a table with some younger girls. He thought it would be good for her to meet some girls, so he just enjoyed watching her while he ate. Even the rubbery macaroni and cheese tasted good when he could look at Melina.

Her image kept him in a cheerful mood all afternoon. He heard the groans around him as teachers assigned extra homework for that night and the weekend, but it didn't bother him at all. He thought maybe he could offer to help Melina with her new classes.

After school, Melina was standing in the parking lot by Clint's truck, waiting for him.

"Really, is it no trouble to take me home?" she asked.

"No trouble at all," Clint said quickly.

As they drove from the parking lot, Clint asked, "So you have foster parents?"

"Yes. They are very nice. They are so good to me. I am so lucky to live with such nice people," Melina said.

"Where are your parents?" Clint asked. "I don't want to be nosy, but I just wondered why you aren't with them."

"My mother is dead. She's been dead a long time. My father too. But my foster parents are very good." Melina smiled at Clint. "You are a very handsome boy. You must have a girlfriend. Would she mind this?" she asked, gesturing at the two of them.

Clint grinned. "I don't have a girlfriend,

so there's nothing to worry about."

He was thrilled that this beautiful girl found him handsome. He could hardly believe his good fortune. Clint had a few girlfriends in the past, but nothing serious.

Clint wanted to ask her again why she was so fearful of the man in the tweed jacket. Something had to be going on. But he decided he wouldn't ask her right away. He didn't want to scare her off. He didn't want to damage what could be a great relationship.

"Turn right here," Melina said, "I live down here."

Clint turned on Wintergreen Avenue and Melina told him to stop before a large old brick apartment building.

After she got out of the truck, Melina turned and said, "Thank you so much for the ride, Clint. I am so happy I met you. I'll see you in class tomorrow, right?"

Melina stood waving as Clint drove away.

But when Clint watched in his rear view mirror, it looked like Melina only pretended to enter the apartment building. She actually turned and walked down an alley. Clint decided she probably lived nearby and was now walking home. For some reason, she didn't want Clint seeing her going into her home.

Clint drove around the block and spotted her coming from the alley and heading for a cluster of old stucco houses. These large houses had probably been nice once, but he could see most of them were in poor repair now. Many of them had been converted to apartments and duplexes. She vanished around a corner. Maybe, Clint thought, she lived in one of those shabby houses and was ashamed of the fact. He'd have to make sure she knew he didn't care where she lived.

Clint was excited about the sudden turn his junior year at Grissom High School had taken. His classes were okay, but he was getting tired of school. He didn't have a girlfriend, and everything was sort of blah. He was anxious for his senior year and then college. But the fact that Melina had come into his life put a fresh, bright glow into the scene. Melina Barja, an exotic little beauty from somewhere far away. She was wonderfully mysterious, and she liked him!

Maybe the fat man in the tweed jacket was just a ruse, Clint thought. Maybe the girl really wanted to meet Clint and she dreamed up the little drama to accomplish that. Clint grinned as he pondered that flattering little thought. Then he realized that was just a fantasy. He had come along at the right time; he had just had the best luck of his life this morning.

Clint's kid sister, Anissa, greeted him as he walked in the door. She was a freshman at Grissom and usually rode the bus or caught a ride from a friend.

"Wow, look at you," Anissa said. "You look like you just won the lottery or something."

"Yeah," Clint said. "I met a really fabulous girl today. And, she seems to really like me."

"She must be cute to get you grinning like that," Anissa said, wrinkling her nose.

....

Clint always watered the flowerbeds at dusk, and today he went outside just before 7:00. He was whistling and feeling good, when from the corner of his eye he noticed a strange car parked across the street. The Asunas lived on a cul-de-sac, and unfamiliar cars were usually around only when somebody was having a party. Clint stared at the dark sedan. A man sat at the wheel. Clint couldn't see much except he looked heavy-set. And he was wearing a tweed jacket.

All kinds of wild theories crowded into Clint's mind. A large man in a tweed jacket was stalking Melina after all! He had seen her get into Clint's truck, so he followed Clint home.

Maybe her parents weren't dead after all. Maybe Melina was the subject of a bitter custody battle between her parents. She might be living with her mother, although her father had legal custody, and they were on the run. Maybe the fat guy was a private detective hired by her father to try to get her back to Europe.

Clint started walking toward the car to talk to the man in the tweed jacket. But as soon as Clint got close, the dark sedan drove away. He apparently did not want to talk to Clint. Not now anyway.

Clint thought about Melina all night. He

had known her for just a day, and already he was worried about her. Clint had heard how vicious those custody battles get sometimes, with kids being kidnapped by one parent and forced from the parent they want to be with. Clint couldn't wait for morning when he'd see Melina again. Maybe she'd feel comfortable enough with him now to tell him the truth about what was going on.

....

In the morning, Clint parked his truck and hurried to his biology class. Dale and Ricky were already standing there talking about last night's NBA game.

Clint looked around, hoping Melina would be early. A few minutes later, she came walking up. She was wearing black pants and a yellow pullover, and she looked even more beautiful than she had yesterday. Her long, shiny black hair flowed down her back like a dark, mysterious river.

"Hi, Clint," Melina said cheerfully. She was smiling as if she didn't have a worry in the world, but then, suddenly, the smile was ripped from her face and panic took its place. Clint thought she had seen something out on the street. She turned and ran toward the restrooms without a word. She was hurrying so fast she almost stumbled and fell. Clint looked out onto the street. He saw the back end of a dark sedan going around the corner.

2

MELINA RETURNED to the classroom before biology class began. She slipped in, smiled at Clint, and sat down.

Ms. Reynosa lectured on new advances in gene research. Clint loved science and he was good at it, but Melina looked perplexed, as if she weren't getting much from the lecture.

Right after class ended, Clint hurried to her side and said, "We could eat lunch together and talk about science, if you need help."

"Oh, Clint, that would be wonderful," Melina said.

"Uh, Melina, I couldn't help noticing you got scared right before class started," Clint said. "What frightened you? Was it the man in the dark sedan?"

"Oh, many things frighten me, I'm afraid. It is because of the conditions in my country, where I grew up. The wars and all," Melina said sadly.

"That same car was in front of my house last night, Melina. I just want you to know that if there's something bothering you, you can talk to me about it, okay?" Clint said.

Melina's large eyes widened. "It is okay. I'm sure it's nothing," she said.

"Melina, you know that it's against the law for people to hassle other people in this country. If there's somebody hassling you, you can call the police and they'll help," Clint said.

"The police? No no," Melina said quickly. "No, I would not want to call the police."

Clint knew there were countries in the world where people feared the police as an arm of the brutal government. They feared the police more than they even feared criminals. People coming from those places often had a hard time understanding how it was in the United States.

"Melina, the police here are nice. They help people," Clint said.

"I know," Melina said, "but never call them for me. You must promise me, Clint."

Clint nodded slowly. "If that's what you want. But you seemed to be scared of the guy in the tweed jacket and the guy in the dark sedan. Maybe it was the same guy. I hate to see you afraid like that," he said.

Melina smiled. "It is all right. This country is so new to me that I am nervous. I keep remembering old, bad things. But I will soon forget them, and then nothing will frighten me. You must be patient with me, Clint," she said.

In English, Dale and Ricky descended on Clint with questions.

"How did you get that babe eating out of your hand like that?" Dale demanded.

"She's so gorgeous, she looks like she should be on television or something," Ricky said.

"I helped her out a bit yesterday. I guess she just likes my type," Clint said, grinning.

"It just doesn't make sense, man," Dale grumbled. "She looks at you like you're some kind of an idol or something."

Melina joined Clint for lunch, but she didn't buy a meal in the cafeteria. She brought a thermos of hot soup that she poured into a little plastic bowl from her backpack. Then she took out a sandwich.

"So, you found out how bad the cafeteria food is, huh?" Clint joked. "You're brown-bagging it!"

"No, I think it must be very good. Your meal looks . . . good. What is it?" Melina asked, staring at Clint's lunch tray.

"It's called macaroni salad," Clint said.

"Oh. I thought macaroni was pasta. But if it is a salad, it must be a vegetable," Melina said.

"No, it is pasta. But there are vegetables hidden somewhere in this mess," Clint said.

"Well, it is probably good, but my mother, my foster mother, she makes lunches for me, and it would be impolite if I would not eat them," Melina said.

Ricky brought his tray over to join them. Ricky dug his elbow into Clint's side and looked meaningfully at Melina. Clint sighed and introduced the two of them. Melina smiled at Ricky and said, "If you are a friend of Clint's then you must be very nice too, because he is wonderful."

"Melina. That's such a pretty name,"

Ricky said. "A pretty name for a pretty girl."

"How nice you are!" Melina said.

"What part of the world do you come from, Melina?" Ricky asked.

For just a second Melina looked bewildered, then she said, "Italy. I am from Italy."

Right away Clint thought there was something fishy here. She had explained her fear of the man in the tweed jacket by saying conditions in her own country were so frightening that she had grown afraid of everything. She had mentioned wars. But in Italy? Clint's family had visited Italy and the Mediterranean last year, and he knew no wars had taken place since World War II.

"Italy, eh?" Ricky said. "Is it true that in Italy guys pinch pretty girls they see on the street?"

Melina looked confused. "I don't know. I mean, we lived in a small town where nothing much happened," she said.

"You look Italian," Ricky said. "That great olive skin and dark hair."

"Oh, thank you," Melina said.

When Ricky left, Clint offered to take Melina home from school again today. "Oh thank you so much, but today my father—my foster father—he is picking me up. But it is so kind of you to ask," she said.

Clint was disappointed that he wouldn't be taking Melina home today. He had just about worked up enough courage to ask her if she'd want to stop for a pizza or something. Clint was dejected later as he walked to his truck to go home.

"Excuse me," a man said. He stepped from a dark sedan parked nearby on the street. He was wearing a dark sweater.

"Yeah?" Clint answered. "What can I do for you?"

"I'm a private detective, and I need to talk to the girl that was with you yesterday. Her name is Melina Barja. Would you know her address?" he asked.

The man was one of those people with almost no neck. Clint knew a couple of guys at Grissom High who played football and looked a little like that already. Maybe when they got older like this guy, their necks would disappear and their heads would sit on their shoulders too. The man also had small, intense eyes like a bird of prey circling patiently over a hot summer field looking for something to seize and eat. Clint did not like the man.

"I don't know her address," Clint said coldly. "What is this about anyway?"

"Well, I'm working for a client and of course it must remain confidential," the man said.

"Are you following the girl around?" Clint asked in a hostile voice. "You know, there are some pretty strict laws against stalking. If I were you, I'd back off before I got in trouble, mister."

The heavy man smiled. "I was in the Los Angeles Police Department for 25 years. I know the law," he said.

"Yeah? Well, I notice you're not with them anymore, so maybe you overstepped the bounds somewhere along the line," Clint said. "Just leave the girl alone. If you've got some client who's interested in contacting her, write her a letter in care of the school or something. Don't stalk her and frighten her, okay?"

Clint was surprised at how angry he felt. He was feeling very protective of

Melina Barja even though he had met her only the day before.

The man walked back to his dark sedan and drove a short distance down the street. Clint figured he would wait until his truck was in motion and then he would tail Clint, hoping Clint would lead him to Melina. Clint smiled to himself as he pulled from the school parking lot. The large man thought Clint was a fool, but he would soon learn otherwise.

The guy was a pro. He didn't immediately gun his engine and follow Clint. He waited a while. He waited until Clint had turned the corner and didn't get behind him until there was a line of cars between them. But after Clint made a few turns, he noticed the guy was there.

Clint drove to the opposite end of town, into a nice neighborhood of upscale condominiums. He parked and walked up to one of the condos. Then he slipped down a walkway and came around the back of his truck. He saw the dark sedan parked at the end of the street under a large, spreading Brazilian pepper tree. Clint figured the private detective was probably already looking in the condo development for Melina.

By the time the man returned to his sedan, Clint had driven away. Clint was delighted by how he had fooled the guy.

But Clint had to find out what was going on. Why did the detective want Melina's address? What was Melina hiding? Where did she live? Clint had to find out. If Melina didn't level with Clint, then how could he help her?

3   WHEN HE WAS SURE he was no
     longer being followed, Clint drove
     back to the neighborhood where
he had dropped Melina off yesterday. The
private detective would be nosing around
the condominiums for a long time, and he
would have no idea where Clint had gone.

Clint drove down an alley to the cluster
of duplexes he had seen before. It was not
a good neighborhood. Many of the roofs
on the houses were in terrible shape.
Patches of various colors appeared on the
walls of some of the stucco houses

Clint stopped at a green stucco house,
its front yard bare except for a cluster of
cacti. He rang the bell, and an elderly
woman came to the door.

"I'm looking for Melina Barja," Clint
said.

"No hablo ingles," the woman said.

"Me llamo Clint," Clint said. "Donde
esta Melina Barja?"

"Ah," the woman said, pointing to a

small house at the end of the street.

It was getting late; darkness was descending. Clint needed to get home before his family started to worry. He hurried toward the small house the woman had pointed out, hoping to find Melina there. He needed her to be honest with him. Why was that guy following her? What was going on in her life?

As Clint reached the house, a man appeared alongside the garage. He looked about 40. He had unruly dark hair and bushy eyebrows. Clint wondered if he might be Melina's foster father.

"Hi," Clint said. "Does Melina Barja live here?"

The man glared at Clint. "Get out of here," he barked.

The man had thick, muscular arms that strained at the T-shirt he was wearing.

"Look, I'm a friend of hers. I just want to talk to her," Clint tried to explain.

The man took an aggressive step toward Clint. "I said to get out of here," he growled.

"Excuse me, mister, but who are you?" Clint asked.

"I told you to get lost, punk. Don't you understand English? Or maybe you'd like a broken nose. Is that what you're looking for? I can give it to you real easy."

Clint was already 6 feet tall. He was well built too. He didn't like being bullied by a guy like this.

"Look, man, you've got no right to tell me I can't talk to a friend who lives in this house. Melina Barja is a friend, and I'd just like to talk to her," he said.

"I am Melina's brother, and I look out for her," the man said. "If you are not gone in two minutes, I'm going to break your neck."

Her brother? Clint was shocked. He didn't know what to do. He was afraid something had happened to Melina in that house. Maybe she was being held against her will by this thug and his friends claiming to be her relatives.

Clint felt like calling the police and asking them to check up on Melina's safety. But then he remembered the pleading in her eyes and the desperation in her voice. *The police? No no . . . I would not want to call the police . . .*

*never call them for me. You must
promise me, Clint.*

Clint finally retreated and went walking
back down the street toward his pickup.
He was sick to his stomach at the thought
that the brutal-looking man he had just
talked to had anything to do with Melina.
Was that thug one of the men stalking
Melina? Or was he really Melina's brother?

Clint called home from his cell phone.
He told his mom he wouldn't be home for
a couple of hours. He said something
about working on a science project with
Dale. He didn't want to worry his mother
by telling her what he was really doing.
How could he explain that he was so
worried about this girl he had only known
for a short time that he couldn't come
home tonight without knowing she was
safe? His mom would tell him in no
uncertain terms that he had no business
sticking his nose into something that
might be dangerous.

Clint sat in his truck for about an hour
in the darkness. Then he walked slowly
down the street. There were lights
glowing in all the small houses as people

came home and dinners were started.

When Clint got to Melina's house, he hid himself in a thicket of eucalyptus trees, hoping for some glimpse of her. That would reassure him. After a while he heard talking coming from the house. He heard a woman's voice and then a man's voice. Somebody laughed. It did not sound like there was a band of criminals in the house holding Melina hostage.

Maybe, Clint thought, the creepy man was supposed to marry Melina, which would make him angry if a young male showed up looking for her. He might have been chosen to be the one to ask for Melina's hand in marriage. In some cultures, older men married much younger girls. Poor Melina, Clint thought. How terrible it would be if that girl were forced to marry somebody like that nasty-tempered thug. What an awful life she would have.

The door to the house opened, and Clint shrank back into the leafy branches of the tree. Melina came outside. She was alone. She had changed into a little blue dress, and she was barefoot. She stood for a moment in the doorway, her arms folded. Her long hair blew around her face, making feathery patterns on her smooth, lovely cheeks.

Clint felt goosebumps popping out all over his body. She was so beautiful. So tender, sweet, and beautiful. He ached with the thought of her.

"What are they?" she asked back over her shoulder to someone in the house.

"Nighthawks or maybe owls," a woman said.

"Oh, they're so beautiful," Melina said. "Flying free. I love wild birds. Birds in a cage are the saddest things in the world." She didn't seem to be afraid.

Clint waited until she went inside again, closing the door after her. Then he started for home. He had satisfied himself that she was okay. Those questions he wanted to ask her could wait until Monday.

When Clint got home, his sister was sprawled in the living room watching television. "Did that beauty queen hang with you again today?" she asked Clint.

"Yeah. I think we've got something going," Clint said.

Anissa laughed. "She probably just wants you to help her with science," she said.

....

The first thing Clint did when he got to school on Monday was to look for Melina. She was early, waiting outside the biology lab. She was the only student there.

"Hi, Melina. How are you?" Clint asked. He didn't look forward to telling her he was nosing around her house, but he wanted to ask about the thug who claimed to be her brother.

"I am very good," Melina said. "Already I like biology better because of you."

"Melina," Clint asked bluntly, "do you have a boyfriend?"

She giggled. "I think so," she said. "I think you are him, Clint."

"M-Me?" Clint stammered.

"Yes, you are my boyfriend. I think so," she said.

"That's . . . uh . . . great," Clint said. He wasn't sure what to make of her saying he was her boyfriend, but he couldn't ask her about the guy claiming to be her brother now. He just couldn't.

When lunchtime came, Clint was alone with Melina. It was a good opportunity for some serious conversation.

"Melina, I'm kind of worried about you. This guy was asking me for your address. He said he was a private detective. I didn't tell him anything. Then he followed me, thinking I was going to your house or something. I drove around and around, and I lost him. But it's so hard being worried about you and not knowing what's going on. Could you just clue me in?" he said.

Melina looked sad for a few minutes, then she said, "Clint, after school, maybe we could go to some quiet place and talk. Maybe we could go to the beach and talk. Then you will understand."

"Good," Clint said.

....

After school, Clint bought some tacos and sodas from Pedro's Taco Shop on the corner, and he and Melina drove down to the beach. It was a cool, cloudy day; the sand was empty except for two sandpipers who ran into the water, then raced the incoming tide back to shore.

"I don't want to pry into your life, Melina, but if I'm going to help you, I need to know what's going on," Clint said.

"You are so nice," Melina said. "I feel so lucky that we met a few days ago."

She and Clint sat on a big beach towel, and for a few minutes, Melina just sat there scraping patterns in the wet sand with her finger, as if she were gathering the courage to talk.

She made circles and pyramids and then, abruptly, she stopped and looked up at Clint. "I am going to be very rich when I am 18. I am now 16½. So there are 1½ years yet. I cannot imagine such a thing happening, but it's true."

"Wow," Clint said, wondering silently why she was living under such humble circumstances now if she was an heiress.

"You see, my grandfather was very rich. In Greece. He had as much money as some small countries have. When he died, he left all his money to my mother. My father was already dead. My mother was a young widow. Then this man, this evil, greedy man, came along, and he married her. I was about four when he became my stepfather. Our life was so horrible. This man married my mother only for her money. He is a horrible, evil man, Clint. When I was 14, my mother . . . " the girl paused and swallowed hard. "My mother died. She was walking with him, with my stepfather, along the cliffs. They say she lost her footing and fell . . ."

Clint put his hand gently on the girl's shoulder. She wiped tears away and went on. "I think maybe she did not fall. I think maybe he pushed her . . . " Melina said brokenly.

Clint felt numb. His mind began to race ahead. He began to understand.

4 "DIDN'T THE POLICE investigate your mother's death?" Clint asked.

"No. Everything is corrupt there. We lived on an island off Greece. My stepfather is very powerful. He bought off the police. The police are very crooked there. I had a nice nanny; she and her husband took care of me. It is them who are now my foster parents. You see, Clint, my mother was beginning to fear the man she married. She set up her will in a special way. She gave her husband control of the money until I am 18. But he cannot spend more than the trustees allow. When I am 18, all the money comes to me, billions and billions," Melina said.

She took a deep breath before going on. "So my stepfather must get me back to the island before I turn 18. Then I am a prisoner, like a bird in a cage. I think then I will die like my mother in an accident that is not really an accident."

"Melina, do you think your stepfather

has sent that guy who's stalking you?" Clint asked.

"Yes. They are watching me, waiting for their chance. But they will not harm me. They will try to somehow kidnap me and take me back to the island. But if I die before I am 18, my mother's will says that my stepfather will get nothing, and it will all go to charity. So, you see, they cannot kill me. They can only watch me and, if possible, take me back to the island. When I am there I will be a prisoner until I am 18 and inherit the money, and then I think it is over for me. My nanny and her husband knew all this, and they helped me escape to the United States," Melina said.

"Melina, we've got to do something," Clint said.

"I am very careful. Those who watch me hope to talk to me. To try to convince me to go home. They tell many lies. They will say my stepfather loves me and misses me. But I know the truth," Melina said.

"You think the guy in the tweed jacket was trying to talk to you?" Clint asked.

"Yes. I recognized his face from the

island where I lived. They will stop at nothing. They will say my stepfather is dying and he wants to ask my forgiveness. If they get me back there, it is all over for me," Melina said.

For a moment or two, Clint wondered if this story Melina was telling him was all true. The poor little rich girl fleeing from her wicked stepfather and taking refuge in a poor neighborhood in the United States.

"Melina, all this sounds so incredible," Clint said.

"You do not believe me?" she asked with a stricken look.

"Oh sure, yes, absolutely," Clint said quickly. "I believe you." But he didn't, not totally.

Melina opened her purse. She drew out a beautiful brooch made of large diamonds surrounded by magnificent rubies.

Clint sucked in his breath. His father was a jeweler. Although Clint was not an expert like his father, he had spent many hours in the store. His father had explained many times how to verify the value of a piece and individual gems. Clint knew this brooch was genuine.

"This is all I have of value. It is from my mother. She had many like this. She gave this to me on my 13th birthday," she said.

"Wow, that's gorgeous, Melina. But isn't it dangerous to carry it around? Shouldn't it be in a vault?" Clint asked.

Melina smiled. "I wanted you to see it so you'd know I am truthful. I was once rich, and if I get to my 18th birthday free, I shall be again. If I were not telling you the truth about my rich Greek grandfather, then where would a poor girl like me get such an expensive brooch?" she asked.

The sky was turning pink. Soon it would be scarlet, then blue, and the colors would finally fade into darkness. But right now there was a pink glow on everything that made Melina even more beautiful.

"I want to get an American school education," Melina said. "I want to be like a regular person until I am 18. It will be the first time in my life I am in classes with people my age. When I was small, I lived in a big, old house with servants. I got all my education from old tutors. It was not fun at all. Now I am so excited I will be going to football games."

Clint smiled at the bubbly enthusiasm Melina displayed, wanting with all his heart to believe her.

"I am so lucky now," she said, her eyes shining. "I can dance. I can be with my friends. I have interesting classes, and I have a boyfriend!"

Clint couldn't help smiling at her. He couldn't help feeling happy for her too. But he was still concerned about her. What she said was almost impossible to believe. But if it was true, she needed someone watching out for her. Either way, Clint had some thinking to do.

"Listen, Melina. If your stepfather has people looking for you, you . . . we . . . need to be careful. I'm going to write down my cell phone number for you. Keep it with you. Do you have a cell phone?" When Melina shook her head, Clint went on. "It's not important. If something happens, find a phone. Any phone. Knock on someone's door if you have to. I'll always have my phone on so you can reach me, okay?"

"Okay," Melina answered. "But, I'm sure it will be all right. I am very careful. My foster father and mother watch out for me too."

Clint drove Melina to the apartment building, and she pretended to go in as she had before. Then she hurried down the alley to the house where she really lived. Clint thought she would soon be comfortable enough with him to tell him where she really lived and to introduce him to her foster parents.

That evening, Clint told his parents about Melina Barja. He told them the strange story she had told him.

Clint's father was a hardheaded businessman. He had spent a couple decades telling the difference between fake jewels and the real thing. He had become a skeptic. Both Clint's father and grandfather were gemologists, experts in the science of gemstones. They graded and judged thousands of pieces. Now Clint's grandpa was retired, and his dad fashioned jewelry pieces for an exclusive shop in Los Angeles.

When his dad heard Melina's story, he

got a skeptical look on his face and he said, "Clint, I think the girl is handing you a line. A girl being threatened by some wicked stepfather like that would be hiding in some secure location with bodyguards, not running around a high school here."

His mom was more romantic and trusting, but she agreed. "Probably your little friend has a great imagination. I went to school with a girl named Desiree, and she was always telling us her mother was some famous actress and her grandfather was a justice of the Supreme Court. They were all lies," his mom said.

"But Melina is so sincere, you guys," Clint argued. "You've really got to believe her . . . "

"And she is undoubtedly beautiful too," his dad said, "which makes it much easier for a guy to believe her."

"But, Dad," Clint argued, "there *are* guys watching her. I've seen this big guy myself. He was trying to wheedle her address from me. If it's all just Melina's imagination, then who was that big, burly guy talking to me?"

Clint's dad smiled. "Well Clint, enjoy being with her. If she said she was from Mars, you'd probably believe her. Enjoy the ride, son, but keep your seatbelt fastened. You might be heading for a bumpy landing down the road," he said.

"She really likes me, Dad," Clint said. "She says I'm her boyfriend and she's so lucky to have met me. She says that over and over."

His mom laughed. "Well, who knows?" she said. "If she really is an heiress, you could end up with a very rich sweetheart, Clint. Just think of it! If the friendship lasts, you could be one of those rich young couples having holidays on the Riviera. Maybe with a hideaway in the South Pacific."

"I hope you'll occasionally invite your parents to visit you there," his dad said, his eyes twinkling with disbelief.

Clint couldn't get Melina off his mind all evening. If her story was true, then he felt sorry for her. How terrible to live with an evil stepfather and then have your mother die under suspicious circumstances. If that was what actually happened, then

Melina was coping with it all amazingly well.

....

The next afternoon, Clint, Ricky, and Dale were on their way to look at a used car for Dale. They were going to check out a Volkswagen that Dale's neighbor was selling.

"I've always wanted a VW, and this sounds like a great ride," Dale said.

They were listening to the radio when the music was interrupted by a news bulletin.

"About 45 minutes ago, a man was shot in his car, which was parked near Gus Grissom High School. School was over for the day, and there were few students on campus, except for members of the basketball team and glee club. No injuries were reported among any of the students, although several clearly heard the shots and ran for cover. Police are not yet saying that proximity to Grissom High was connected in any way to the shooting. There have been no reports of recent gang activity near Grissom High, though several years ago a drive-by shooting took place a block away. Police are not releasing the name of the victim. Unconfirmed reports are that he was killed. Stay tuned for updates on this breaking story."

"Wow, a guy murdered on the street in front of our school," Dale said. "No place to hide, huh?"

"I wonder if a student shot him," Ricky said. "I hope not. Maybe the guy was a teacher and the kid was mad about a bum grade."

Clint was thinking in another direction. He was remembering the man with no neck sitting in the dark sedan near Grissom High the other day. Could he have been the man who was shot? And did it have anything to do with Melina? Clint began to feel scared.

Clint tried to convince himself that the dead man was not the guy who was stalking Melina. He concentrated on helping Dale check out the Volkswagen. The boys looked at the engine and checked the tires and the upholstery. Everything seemed nearly perfect.

"Grab it, man," Clint advised Dale. "You'll never get another deal like this."

But as hard as Clint tried to immerse himself in the car deal, he kept wondering about the dead man and hoping it was not the neckless guy.

By evening the television news programs were giving major coverage to the shooting. The victim had been identified as Edgar Sandusky, a private investigator from San Francisco. Clint stared at the television screen as a poor photograph of the man came on. Clint turned numb. He wasn't absolutely sure, but the photo looked like the guy who asked Clint for Melina's address. He looked quite a bit younger, but the face was the same. Clint was pretty sure it was the same guy.

The television reporter was talking about gang activity near the school and interviewing the concerned parents of the kids who had been at the school when the shooting took place. Then they interviewed a shaken little sophomore from the glee club.

"It's like so weird," the girl said. "I saw the guy sitting in his car, right? I mean, like there he was and I saw him. And then I went to practice and I hear these shots, right? Bang, bang, bang, like firecrackers, you know? And like he's dead. Is that weird or what? I mean, I've never seen a guy like that one minute and then he's dead. It's like I am totally freaked out, you know?"

Clint's mind went into a spin. If somebody shot the guy stalking Melina, then what was going on? Were there criminals on her side too? He wondered what he was getting into. Clint did not mention anything to his parents about a connection between the dead man and Melina. But he spent a sleepless night. Somewhere in this mysterious girl's life, there were people willing to commit murder, and that was terrifying.

5 MELINA SEEMED distraught when Clint saw her at school the next morning. She appeared close to weeping all during biology, and when Clint approached her after class, she whispered, "later," and dashed away.

Finally, at lunchtime, Clint caught up to Melina. She seemed more composed now. They were both brown-bagging it, so they went to a quiet place under a pepper tree to eat.

"Clint, I was so frightened when I heard what happened to that man," Melina said. "I was sick. I could not eat. I could not sleep. I am still shaking," Melina said.

"Melina, if he was hired by your stepfather, then who killed him?" Clint asked.

"He was not doing his job. He was supposed to kidnap me and take me home before now. He had failed. But he knew too much. My stepfather has sent other, worse men after me. Killers!" Melina said.

"Melina, I'm finding all this really tough to digest. I mean if there are murderers after you, you've got to go to the police. This is getting serious," Clint said.

Melina put her face in her hands and wept.

"It is the dark and evil world I come from, Clint," Melina cried. "It is a world you know nothing of."

"What are you talking about?" Clint asked.

"The organized criminals. My stepfather is a drug dealer, and he works with organized criminals. The one who brings me home will be rewarded with a great amount of money. So these bad men are vying to do this. I think this man, Sandusky, was killed by another of the criminals my stepfather has hired . . . " Melina said.

"Melina, listen to me. You've got to go to the police right now," Clint said. "There's been a murder. You have to talk to the police about what you know."

Melina's eyes filled with tears. She reached up and put her hands on Clint's shoulders, bringing him closer to her. He heard her breath coming in frightened gasps.

"Clint, I am only 16. I am legally a child. My stepfather is my legal guardian. He has the right to take custody of me. He adopted me when he married my mother. If the police come into this, I will be taken into custody immediately as a runaway child. I will be forced back to my stepfather. I will be like a bird in a cage— he will keep me there until I am 18, and then he will do to me what he did to my mother. Please, Clint. Please help me. I cannot call the police. I cannot," she said.

Clint looked into her tear-filled eyes and he melted. He was scared of what was happening to him. He had always had integrity—he tried to do the right thing, and he knew in his heart that the police needed to know all the details. But it was almost as if Melina had the power to cast a spell over him that clouded his judgment and weakened his moral resolve.

"Okay, okay, Melina. But you're in terrible danger yourself. If these people were willing to kill one of their own, then they might kill you too," he said.

"No, no. They cannot. Then the whole fortune would go to charity. He knows that. My stepfather is very shrewd and cunning. In the last months of my mother's life, she began to see his evil. She made the will so that he could not harm me. Her lawyers did that to protect me until I am 18. That is why I must become 18 here, in this free country," Melina said.

"I'm just so confused," Clint said.

"Today, after school, I will take you to my home. You can meet my foster parents. They will help you to understand, Clint. They can explain better than I can. I have already told them about you—they love you already because you have been such a good friend to me," Melina said.

"Okay, yeah, I'd like to meet them," Clint said. Maybe that would clear things up, he thought. He was now relieved that Melina trusted him enough to take him so completely into her confidence.

All during classes that day, Clint thought about Melina. He was in love with her. He knew that was so stupid because he had known her for such a short time.

But when he looked at her, he turned lightheaded and strange. She was like a fantasy come to life. She was taking over his thoughts and actions, and he didn't care.

Clint drove Melina home the same way they had gone before, but this time she directed him to the stucco house.

"Clint, I was not completely honest with you before. I am ashamed. I pretended I lived in that apartment. Please forgive me. I trusted you, but not with all my heart, but now I do," she said.

When Clint parked in front of the little house, Melina smiled and said, "It is such a humble little house, yes?"

"It looks like home," Clint said.

"You are always so kind. I love that about you, Clint. Some boys would make a cruel joke about such a small place. I am so lucky I met you," Melina said. "When I was younger, I lived in this great house on an island in the Aegean Sea. Did you ever hear of that place?"

"Yeah. The waters are supposed to be the bluest in the world there," Clint said. "Last summer our family took a vacation in Greece. I loved it."

"Well, I grew up in a huge house. There were too many rooms to count. Servants did everything. You would think that is so wonderful, but it is not. All the beautiful furniture and the fine clothing and the jewels do not matter when there is darkness inside the house. My stepfather was cruel to my mother and me. It is much better in this little house with people who are kind and good," Melina said.

Melina took Clint inside the two-bedroom house. The furniture was pleasant but obviously inexpensive.

"Nanny, this is the boy I told you about," Melina said to a woman who looked in her late thirties. She was slim and attractive with her dark curly hair showing a few strands of gray. She had a lovely oval face and expressive eyes.

"Hello," the woman said. "I am Irini and my husband—I am so sorry he could not be here—his name is Hyma. I am so thankful that you have become Melina's friend. Ever since Melina was a baby, we have cared for her. I was her nursemaid when I was just a child myself. We feel like she is our own child."

Clint sat down at the table. Melina served him some strong coffee and sweet rolls filled with nuts and raisins. Irini sat opposite him, her expression intense.

"Melina has told you of the problem, yes?" she asked.

"She told me her stepfather wants her back so he can control her until she's 18, so he can get the inheritance from her," Clint said.

Irini nodded. "It is so. He is a very bad man. He is a criminal, but the police will not touch him. He is too powerful. He hires men to try to bring Melina back. They have told Melina lies. That her stepfather truly loves her and will treat her nice this time. But they are all lies. Once she is in his clutches, she is doomed," Irini said, a woeful expression in her eyes.

"Melina thinks that guy who was shot outside the school the other day was working for her stepfather," Clint said.

"Yes, but there is no honor among thieves. He did not serve his purpose anymore, so they got rid of him," Irini said.

When Clint left the house, he felt better. Irini seemed very sincere. Clint wanted to believe Melina's story, and meeting Irini had made it easier.

....

The shooting of Edgar Sandusky remained top news for several days. Since it had happened at the edge of a neighborhood where gang activity was not unusual, that was the angle the police seemed to be pursuing. Clint was torn with remorse that he knew more about the crime than the police did and yet he was keeping silent. He had never done anything like that before, and he felt guilty.

The stories did not mention a criminal connection linked to Sandusky. He was apparently a single man, with no family ties, who had come from San Francisco to locate some missing jewelry. That was what the news reports said. Clint assumed the jewelry story was a cover for what Sandusky was really doing, shadowing Melina.

The guilt that tormented Clint was

unrelenting. Because Sandusky had been a police officer for many years, a lot of police officers came to pay their respects at his funeral. Clint was watching the service on television when his mother joined him.

"It's always so touching to watch services for police officers," his mom said. "There is such a brotherhood among those officers. His brothers and sisters have come to honor him now. Look at all those uniforms . . . Isn't that nice? Clint?"

"Yeah," Clint said. He continued to stare at the television screen.

The motorcycle officers were leading the hearse. Clint wondered how Sandusky could have inspired so much support among all those good people. After all, he had quit the police force to become a hired goon for some foreign drug dealer who was trying to kidnap his daughter. It didn't make sense.

A lot of things didn't make sense, and they were driving Clint crazy. He wished he didn't care so much for Melina. He wished he could just look at the whole situation with clear-eyed and disinterested honesty. But since the day he met her, he thought about her constantly.

He kept picturing how she looked standing in the doorway of the little house that night, in the little blue dress, barefoot, her black hair blowing around her hauntingly lovely face. Clint was addicted to her. Yes, he thought miserably, that was the word for it. He was addicted, and he couldn't act in the way his conscience and his brains told him to act. Clint kept telling himself that Melina had to be telling him the truth. Irini seemed like a humble, good person. Besides, what other explanation could there be for all this?

6 "DUDE," DALE SAID as he and Clint headed for a basketball game at the downtown arena on Saturday. "How come you look like you have the weight of the world on your shoulders?"

"I keep thinking about that guy who got shot near the school," Clint said.

"Yeah, a good guy like that wasted by gangs," Dale said. "That's what it looks like anyway."

Clint turned and looked at Dale. "You didn't know him, did you? You didn't know Sandusky . . . "

"No, not me, but my uncle is a cop up in Los Angeles," Dale said. "He worked with him. He said there never was a better cop. He had to leave the police department when he had open-heart surgery. I guess being a P.I. is easier work."

Clint felt a fresh rush of guilt.

"You know what really freaks me out?" Dale said as the boys walked into the arena. "The cops have done such a great job cleaning the gangs out of that neighborhood. Since that big sports complex opened up for kids, the skateboard park, the basketball courts, and swimming pools, man, it seemed things were looking up. A lot of the gang wannabes got into sports. It's so creepy that this poor guy gets wasted anyway . . . "

Clint's mouth was dry. He knew he should be telling the police the whole story. Right now they were going down a dead-end street. Clint knew he should be over at the police station right now. He should be explaining how Melina Barja's stepfather had hired Edgar Sandusky to lure her back to the Aegean Sea island and how some other goons had killed the man. But if he did that, then Melina was gone. She was gone from his life, probably forever. Worse yet, such action by Clint could cost the girl her life if what she was telling Clint was the truth . . .

....

Clint invited Melina to his house for Sunday dinner. He said he wanted her to meet his parents. After all, he had met her foster mother.

"So the little girl with the big imagination is coming to dinner," his dad joked. "What's the latest on her travails, Clint?"

His dad was obviously not taking the problem seriously. Of course, he did not know of the connection between Melina's fears and the death of Edgar Sandusky. Clint did not dare tell his parents about that.

"Oh, nothing much new," Clint said. "She just doesn't want to go back home to her stepfather. She kind of thinks he had something to do with her mother's death."

Clint's mom frowned. "Oh, Clint. You didn't tell us that before. That's awful. Why wouldn't the man have been arrested if he harmed the girl's mother?"

"Melina said the police are corrupt where she used to live. When you're rich and powerful you can get away with stuff," Clint said.

"That sounds unlikely," his mom said. "Are you sure this girl doesn't suffer from delusions, Clint?"

"She's okay," Clint said. "And please don't mention any of this stuff to her. She gets upset real easy . . . I guess she's, you know, been through a lot."

"Got it," his dad said. "Nothing controversial."

Clint kept thinking about Edgar Sandusky. If his parents knew what Melina had said about that man's death, they would demand that Clint go to the police. They would not stand still for a moment. Clint kept small secrets from his parents, but he had never kept something this serious from them. It worried him. It made him feel bad.

When Clint picked Melina up at her house, she was wearing a peach colored pullover and loose pants made out of some kind of stretchy fabric. Her long black hair was gathered in a bun at the nape of her neck. She looked much older than 16. But she looked as lovely as ever.

"You look great, Melina," Clint said, thinking how proud he would be to introduce this girl to his parents. When he was with Melina, all his fears and doubts vanished. There was nothing but Melina.

"Thank you, Clint," Melina said. "I don't want you to be ashamed of me!"

Clint laughed. How could he ever be ashamed of a girl like this?

When Clint brought Melina into his living room, his mom greeted her with a hug. Clint's mom greeted every guest with a hug. She was a very loving person.

Anissa said, "Hi, Melina."

Clint's dad smiled and said, "We're really glad you could come for dinner, Melina. We're always glad to meet Clint's friends, but I've got to say, you're the prettiest one yet!"

"Oh," Melina said, "you are so sweet, so nice. I am not surprised though that Clint has such nice parents. He is so kind to me. I think he must come from a fine family."

Clint's mother served marinated sirloin tips, baked potatoes, and string beans with her special onion sauce for dinner.

"Clint tells us you're Italian," his dad said. "Last summer we passed through Italy and went to Greece. We had a great time."

"It is very beautiful there," Melina said.

"We tried not to get bogged down in the

touristy stuff," Clint's dad continued. "We tried to get the flavor of the country by asking the locals for good places to eat. We met some very nice people."

"Italians are warm-hearted people," Melina said.

"So, Melina, how do you like Grissom High School?" his mom asked. "It must be quite a change for you."

"Oh yes. Like I told Clint, I was tutored at home. I did not go to a classroom at all. It was very lonely. I like the high school. It is so exciting. It is full of life. And Clint helps me over the rough spots," Melina said.

After dinner, Clint and Melina went outside to sit in the little gazebo where his mom's roses climbed on the trellis walls.

"What a pretty yard you have," Melina said.

"Yeah, Mom is real artistic. She planted all the roses and even made the little koi pond over there," Clint said.

"She must work many hours here. She does not have a job?" Melina asked as she settled herself in the porch swing.

"She's a cellist in the city symphony.

But she loves beautiful plants as much as she loves beautiful music. She's one of the most loving people I've ever met," Clint said. He wanted Melina to feel comfortable with his family. He hoped she would come to see them as trustworthy.

"Oh, how nice. You have such nice parents," Melina said. "It must be wonderful . . ." her voice trailed.

Clint felt sorry for her again. At times like this, sitting with Melina and looking at her beautiful face, he could not imagine doubting her. The bizarre details of her story seemed perfectly normal at such times. When Clint was away from her, he was tormented by doubts, but not now. Now his heart ached with sympathy for this poor girl who had lost both her parents and was now threatened by an evil, greedy stepfather.

Suddenly Melina leaned forward in the swing and put her hands on Clint's shoulders. She kissed him gently on the lips. Clint felt as if he had been transported to some magical kingdom.

"Melina," he gasped.

"I hope you do not think I am a forward

person, Clint, but I care for you so much. You have treated me as if we have known each other all our lives, and yet we were strangers just a short time ago. I am so lucky to meet you. And now you bring me to your home like this and I am touched," Melina said.

"It . . . it was a . . . wonderful kiss," Clint stammered losing all his cool. He felt like he was back in junior high dancing with Michelle Obermann, who had been a foot taller than he was.

When they went back inside, Melina said, "Mr. Asuna, you have been so kind to me, I am ashamed to ask a favor. But Clint told me I should not be carrying this brooch around, that it should be in a safe. I was wondering, do you have a safe where you could keep this for me?" She drew out the brooch with its diamonds and rubies. "It was a gift to me from my mother before she died."

Clint's father looked at the brooch for a moment. "Do you mind if I look at this under a microscope, Melina?" he asked.

The girl shook her head. Clint's dad took the brooch over to his powerful microscope to examine it.

Then he said, "Clint is right. This is a magnificent piece. It is extremely valuable. If you want, I'll keep it in our hall safe as long as you need. I have a large hall safe for the pieces that I design for work. But you really should get a safe-deposit box at the bank."

"Oh, I will do that. But if you would just keep it for a few days, I would be so grateful," Melina said. Melina watched as Clint's dad took the brooch to the hall safe and locked it. "Thank you so much," she said.

Clint drove Melina home. When he returned, he heard his parents talking about her in the kitchen. Clint didn't like to eavesdrop, but he was curious what they had to say about Melina.

"She is a sweet little thing," his mom was saying.

"Too sweet," his dad said. "I'll grant you that she's beguiling, but I get bad vibrations."

"Well, it's her culture, Greg. People from the Old World just seem to have more grace, more manners," Clint's mom said. "We're so used to American teenagers that we think a girl her age is strange when she's so polite."

"Nina, I just don't like Clint getting swept away by someone he's known for such a short time. Did you see how he was smiling at her all through dinner? He seems to be under a spell. Clint is a smart kid, but when it comes to a girl with looks and charm like that, I think he's apt to be foolish," Clint's dad worried.

"Oh, Greg," his mom laughed, "you're making too much of this. Clint has had nice little girlfriends before, and they don't last long. He's 16 years old! How serious can he be when he's 16 years old?"

"I don't know," his dad grumbled. "He's almost 17, and at that age a guy's feelings are pretty strong. I know. I was a kid that age once, and I know how easily I could be influenced."

Clint stiffened. He had to admit, his dad was right. He thought about Melina almost every waking moment. When he wasn't with her, his brain told him her story wasn't logical. But he was very willing to believe her because she seemed so innocent.

Clint turned from the hallway leading to the kitchen. He didn't want his parents to know that he had overheard them talking about him and Melina. And Clint did not want to talk about Melina with his parents either. He knew they had questions. He had questions himself. Clint couldn't answer his own questions. All he knew was that he was crazy about her.

7

WHEN CLINT WENT to school on Monday, he did not see Melina in her usual place waiting for biology class. She was always early. Looking around for her, Clint became nervous wondering if her foster parents were late in dropping her off. Or had something else come up? All kinds of fears attacked him. Maybe one of those thugs her stepfather had hired had succeeded in kidnapping her, and at this moment she was in desperate trouble.

Melina did not appear at all for biology. Clint suffered through the class, unable to concentrate. She had not given him her phone number so he couldn't call to make sure she was all right.

After biology, Clint decided to ditch English and drive to Melina's house. There was no other way. It was madness to think he could go through his day as usual without knowing.

When Clint arrived at the little stucco

house, his heart nearly stopped. There were two police cars parked outside. Clint parked his truck and sat and watched and waited. Finally after 20 minutes the police left, and Clint hurried to the house.

"What's going on?" he asked Irini.

"Come in," Irini said. "Oh, Clint, we were so scared when the police came. Melina escaped out the back door. She is hiding somewhere, but I don't know where. We thought the stepfather had done this. The police were asking us about that man who was shot, that Mr. Sandusky. They asked all kinds of questions. I think they want to blame us for the murder!"

"Did you tell them about Melina's stepfather and how he hired the guy?" Clint asked.

"They would not listen. They want only to blame us," Irini said.

"Are you sure Melina is all right?" Clint asked.

"Yes. Hyma took her. He will find a safe place for us. Hyma is very clever," Irini said.

"When can I see Melina?" Clint asked.

"She will call you when she can, Clint," Irini said.

Clint returned to school, feeling miserable. He forced himself to go through the rest of his classes. Then he rushed home to await Melina's phone call.

"What's the matter, Clint?" Anissa asked him when he walked in. "You look like your dog died."

"I'm expecting an important phone call," Clint said. "Buzz off!"

Anissa looked miffed. "Well, listen to the big sorehead! Did you and your sweetie have a fight or something? Really, Clint, you are so weird since you met that girl. She's a fake if you ask me. I don't trust her," she said.

"She's not a fake," Clint snapped. "She's got real bad problems. You don't know the half of it, squirt. Her parents are dead and . . . "

His cell phone rang. Clint almost fell over his own feet in his haste to get it out of his backpack.

"Clint?" Melina said.

"Melina! I was so worried about you. Are you okay?" Clint asked.

"Yes. The police came to our house. My

foster father hurried me away and we hid. They are trying to blame us for the shooting of that man, Sandusky. It is so awful. My stepfather hired him to kidnap me, and some other thug killed him. Now somehow my stepfather has gotten the police to believe we had something to do with the shooting!" Melina wailed.

"Melina, are you sure of all that? Everything I've heard about Sandusky is good. He was a good cop with a million friends. I don't get it that he turned criminal," Clint said.

"People will do strange things when they are offered a great deal of money. My stepfather is rich and powerful," Melina said. "Clint, would it be possible for me to come to your house for a few days until my foster parents can arrange a safe place for us? I know it is asking a very great favor. I would not blame you for refusing me, but I don't know what else to do." Melina sounded distraught.

"Yeah, of course. We can put you up for as long as you need, Melina. Tell me where you are now, and I'll come get you," Clint said.

"Oh, Clint, thank you. I cannot believe I

am so lucky to have met you. I am at the corner of Briar Street and Manchester where there is a big thrift store. It is not a good place. It is getting dark, and strange men are looking at me. I am frightened," Melina said.

"Hang on, Melina. I'm coming," Clint said.

When Clint hurried toward the garage, Anissa ran after him. "Where are you going, Clint?"

"I've got to pick Melina up. She's going to stay here for a few days. I mean, she's got nowhere else to go," Clint said.

"Here? She's going to live here?" Anissa cried.

"Just get out of my way, okay?" Clint yelled.

"You're not even going to ask Mom and Dad first?" Anissa yelled after him.

"They'll understand," Clint said as he climbed into his truck and gunned the engine.

Clint drove as fast as he legally could to the corner where Melina said she would be waiting. He saw her immediately, trying to shrink into the shadow cast by the thrift store. Clint pulled to the curb, and Melina came running. She had her school backpack, but no luggage.

"Oh, Clint, it is so kind of you to be doing this. I am sorry I am such a bother to you. I didn't know what to do. We cannot stay in the house where we were living, and my foster parents are now working something else out. But they do not want me with them in case the police see me and take me into custody and send me back to the Greek island . . . " she sobbed.

"It's okay," Clint said. "Just relax."

"When the police came, we thought they were coming to take me. Hyma hustled me out the back. I thought, yes, it is the same in this country as it was in mine. There is no justice. The police are the tools of the rich and powerful. I thought I was doomed. I feared they would put me on a plane, and tomorrow I would be in the big, cold house on the island off Greece. There would be no more hope for me. I would be like the bird in the cage that has nothing to look forward to but to die," Melina said as they drove.

Clint reached over and grasped the girl's soft hand. "Don't worry. Nothing like that is going to happen to you. You're going to be fine," he said.

Luckily for Clint, his mom got home before his dad. She was home when Clint and Melina arrived. Clint's mom was a very compassionate person, always ready to lend a helping hand. Besides, she did not ask as many questions as his dad would.

"Mrs. Asuna, I am so sorry to be bothering you like this," Melina said. "Clint said it would be okay for just a day or two. Then my foster parents will have a safe place for us to go."

Clint's mom gave Melina a hug and said, "You stay as long as you need to, sweetheart. We have a nice guest room that's just going to waste most of the time. I mean, we'd be a poor sort of people if we didn't help a friend of our son's."

Clint smiled gratefully at his mother. His mom took Melina to the guest room and closed the door so the girl could freshen up.

"She looks just exhausted," his mom

said. "Poor little thing."

"Thanks, Mom," Clint said. "You're great."

"I don't get it," Anissa muttered. "What's going on here anyway?"

"Melina has a bad family situation," Clint explained. "Her nasty stepfather is trying to drag her back to Greece, and she's afraid for her life."

"Let's all just be gracious to her, Anissa," their mom said. "We can't understand everything about the problem, but we can be gracious."

When Clint's dad came home, he was less understanding than Clint's mom had been.

"Clint, what exactly are we getting involved in?" he asked. "I mean, I'm as willing as the next guy to help someone out who needs it, but this girl's story has more holes in it than Swiss cheese. Her story sounds like something you'd read in a fairy tale. Poor little princess running away from her wicked stepfather with the ogres in pursuit. Come on!"

"I know, Dad. I understand where you're coming from," Clint said. "But I met her foster mom, and she really seemed like a nice lady. If Melina was carrying on some wild fantasy, her foster mother wouldn't be going along with it, would she?"

"The whole thing smells like fish you've left out on the counter too long, Clint," his dad said.

Mr. Asuna had brought home a large bag of diamonds and sapphires for an actress who was staying at a local hotel. Tomorrow morning he would go to the client's room and let her choose the stones that would be used in her wedding tiara and in her rings. Clint's dad put the stones in the wall safe.

That evening, Melina sat with Clint and his parents watching television. His dad only stayed long enough to see the evening news. Then he returned to his sketching table, to get ideas for the pieces he would design for the young actress who had come all the way from France.

Clint's mom always enjoyed classical programs. When she turned on a performance of *Aida* on public broadcasting, Melina remained to listen and watch.

"Ohhhh, opera. I love opera," Melina said.

Clint and his dad didn't like opera, ballet, or, for that matter, symphony music. So his mom's face lit up with delight when Melina was interested.

8 THE NEXT DAY, Clint didn't want to go to school. But when he hinted to his parents that it might be better if he stayed home with Melina, they squashed the plan.

"Melina is a big girl," his mom said. "She can take care of herself."

"No ditching school for frivolous reasons," his dad said even more emphatically.

Clint told Melina to keep all the doors locked and not to open them for anybody except Clint's family.

"I will be fine," Melina assured Clint. "I will be playing on the computer. I love the computer, but my foster parents could not afford one. So I will enjoy playing games and looking stuff up. The time will go so fast until you are home again."

When Clint arrived in biology, Ricky and Dale were waiting for him.

"What happened to the babe?" Dale asked.

"Oh, she's not feeling well," Clint lied. He didn't want to share Melina's strange story with his friends.

"Bet you and her were hanging out yesterday when you ditched school, huh?" Ricky said, with a wink and a grin. "Old Fender hated not seeing you in class. You're one of the few people who actually keeps a discussion going in that boring class. He really missed you."

Clint walked into biology and sat down. Then, in a few minutes, a student came in with a note. Ms. Reynosa read the note and turned to Clint.

"Clint, you need to report to the office," she said.

"Busted!" Dale whispered.

"Detention, man!" Ricky snickered.

Clint walked toward the office, surprised they were making such a big deal out of one absence from English. It was something that students usually worked out with the teacher. But, as Clint drew closer, he noticed three police cars parked outside. Clint put two and two together fast. They were not calling him to the office to talk about missing English class. The police wanted to question him about Melina Barja! What was it that Melina had said . . . ? That they were trying to link her foster parents to the death of Sandusky?

Clint froze, staring at the office, which was still about 50 yards away. If he went in there and they began asking questions, he couldn't give Melina away. Nor could he outright lie to the police. Especially not in a murder investigation. Clint broke out in a cold sweat. He didn't know what to do. If he cooperated with the police, he would have to betray Melina. They would go to his house and take her into custody and eventually deliver her to the man who had legal custody of her—the stepfather she hated and feared.

Clint stood there, breathing hard, remembering Melina's words, *They can only watch me and, if possible, take me back to the island. When I am there I will be a prisoner until I am 18 and inherit the money, and then I think it is over for me* . . .

Clint turned and headed for the student parking lot. He had to get away from here.

He had to warn Melina that she might have to run again, quicker than she had planned to. But before he reached his truck, Clint saw that a police officer was leaning on it. He was waiting for Clint! They had him boxed in. They had to be pretty sure that Clint was tight with Melina and that he could lead them to her!

Clint turned around and rushed from the school onto the street. He had to call Melina and warn her that the police were on his tail and would probably be at the house before long. Clint wished he hadn't left his cell phone in his truck. He had to get to a pay phone. He spotted one outside a drugstore across the street from Grissom High. He rushed to the phone and stuffed the coins into the slot.

When the machine picked up, he spoke loudly, hoping Melina was nearby and would hear the message.

"Melina, this is Clint. Look, I got called from class and the police are swarming all over the school. I think they want to ask me about you. I got away, but they have my truck staked out. I'm afraid when they don't find me here they'll go to my house and find you!" Clint said. "Pick up the phone, Melina!"

He could hear Melina fumbling with the receiver at the other end. "Oh! Clint, stay where you are now. Hyma is here with me. We will come and pick you up. We will be there quickly," Melina said.

Clint was so frightened and confused that he wasn't even sure what was going on. But he did know one thing. He had to avoid being questioned by the police since he knew where Melina was. He couldn't be the one who ratted her out and maybe send her to her death. He loved her too much for that.

Clint waited by the drugstore for about ten minutes until a ratty van pulled up. It cruised slowly to a stop, and Clint spotted Melina in the passenger seat. Clint ran to the van and opened the side door, jumping in. He didn't even see the driver until he was inside and the van was in motion. Then he recognized the man as the one with unkempt hair and bushy eyebrows who claimed to be her brother when he had chased Clint from the house that day.

"Clint, this is Hyma, my foster father,"

Melina said.

"Melina, I met this guy before—he threatened to break my neck!" Clint gasped.

"No, no," Melina said. "It must be a mistake. I think maybe Hyma did not know you were my friend and was trying to protect me, yes?"

"Yeah," Hyma said. "This kid was nosing around the place, and I thought he might be trouble."

"Where are we going?" Clint asked. "I can't hide from the police forever. Maybe you guys should drop me at home and then head for some safe place. If I don't know where you are, Melina, then I can truthfully tell the police that I can't help them . . . "

"Don't worry, Clint," Melina said. "We have it all figured out."

She sounded oddly different. The cute little accent seemed to disappear. Clint couldn't exactly put his finger on it, but she seemed older. The frightened little girl seemed to have aged into a woman. The van was heading for the brushy hill country north of the city.

"Where are we going?" Clint asked again.

His legs had turned numb. He had a terrible, gnawing feeling that something was terribly wrong here.

"Keep your shirt on, kid," Hyma said.

He swerved off the paved road, and they went bouncing down a pathway that was little more than two tire tracks scoured from the dirt. They rounded a corner and there was a lean-to standing under some quaking aspen trees.

"There's a little cabin here," Melina said. "It's a good place to hide. I can hide here until my foster parents find a safe place for us . . . "

Hyma brought the van to a jolting stop. "Why don't you knock it off, babe?" he said.

Clint felt sick to his stomach. "What's going on here?" he demanded.

Hyma and Melina got out of the van. When Clint looked at Hyma, he saw a gun in his hand.

"Out you come, kid," he said.

Clint stared at the gun. He looked at Melina who had walked off a few feet. Her back was turned. Her arms were folded, and she seemed to be staring into the distance. Clint couldn't see her face.

"Melina," Clint said, "what is this? What's going on?"

She may have murmured something about being sorry, or maybe it was just the wind whispering through the quaking aspens.

The man marched Clint into the lean-to. He tied Clint's hands behind his back. Then he tied Clint's ankles together. He stuck a cloth in Clint's mouth and covered his mouth with masking tape.

As Clint lay on the floor bound and gagged, Hyma said, "We're jewel thieves, kid. Old Sandusky was investigating a missing brooch. We had to waste him when he got too close. Now, you stay here nice and quiet. We're going to your house. Irini is there right now. When your parents come home, we'll convince them to open that hall safe and get all those goodies out. Then we'll take your daddy down to his store while Irini is staying with your mom, and we'll get some more goodies. If everybody is nice-nice, then nobody gets hurt."

Clint's brain was swimming in horror and regret. He had been a fool, an idiot. He had believed Melina's fantastic story because she was so beautiful, so charming and vulnerable. But the whole thing was an elaborate ruse to worm her way into the jeweler's family. By befriending Clint, Melina had given her gang access to several million dollars in jewelry.

That was all it was from the beginning. There never was an evil stepfather. Or a great house off an island in Greece. Melina was not Italian, or even a young girl. She was probably a young woman and a hardened criminal.

Clint watched them go to the van and get in. He could see them through the broken window. Melina never looked back.

Clint thought about his parents and Anissa. They would come home, one by one, to be taken hostage by these criminals. They would come to their own house and find it infested with vicious thieves. Irini and Hyma were not gentle foster parents. They were thugs, criminals, like Melina. They were murderers. They had already killed that poor Edgar Sandusky . . .

Somehow, Clint had to get free and tell the police to go to his house. If they went immediately they would find just Irini. If they arrested her, they could wait until Melina and Hyma arrived and arrest them. That would spare Clint's family the horrifying ordeal of being confronted by armed criminals.

This is all my fault, Clint thought miserably as he tugged at the tough ropes binding his wrists. I fell like a fool for a pretty face and believed her nonsense, and now I've put my whole family in jeopardy.

Clint looked around the lean-to, hoping to see some jagged object he could rub his bonds against, to fray the rope. He finally spotted a rusty shovel. If he could roll over there and back up against the sharp edge of the scoop, maybe he could cut his bonds.

Clint used all his strength to maneuver his body into position. He was breathing hard when he finally pushed his bound hands toward the shovel scoop and started sawing the ropes. But then he saw it—the thing coiled beside a garbage pail not more than four feet from the shovel— a snake—a sleeping snake.

If Clint started making noise and maybe knocking things down, the snake would wake up. Clint couldn't tell if it was a rattlesnake, but most of the snakes in these hills were. If the rattler struck before Clint had freed himself, he would have no way of getting help. He would die here. But still he couldn't just remain quiet and allow what was about to happen to his family take place. He had to risk rousing the rattlesnake. He had to.

9 CLINT BEGAN SAWING his ropes against the shovel scoop. He nicked his wrist and the pain shot up his arm. He kept at the effort, ignoring the pain. He thought about the police back at Grissom High School. He wondered how soon they would realize he had fled the school. How long before they would go to his house and try to talk to him there? He hoped it would happen fast. Then, even if he didn't get free in time to call the police, maybe they would get to the house before his parents got home to be confronted by the criminals. But if the police rapped on the door, Irini simply wouldn't answer. And the police would probably go away and return much later. Clint's family could still be in great danger . . .

Clint glanced at the sleeping snake. It had not moved yet. Clint worked more feverishly, scraping the rope binding his wrists against the shovel. Sticky blood now oozed from the gashes he was making in his wrists. Every couple of minutes, Clint yanked at the ropes, hoping to find them weakened enough to yield. Then he would saw at them with even more fury, ignoring the throbbing pain and the blood running down his hands. Finally the rope yielded, and Clint freed his hands.

Clint glanced at the snake that was not yet stirring. He ripped off the masking tape and spat out the cloth in his mouth. He sawed the ropes from his ankles, using a rusty screwdriver he found. Clint looked at his watch. It was past noon. He felt hopeful. The earliest anyone got home at his house was 2:30. His mom got home from symphony practice then. Next came Anissa and finally his dad. Clint felt he now had a good chance to get the police to the house before his family was confronted.

Clint ran down the dirt road to the asphalt highway. There wasn't a lot of traffic here, but he was sure there would be some vehicle in the next five to ten minutes. If he walked down the highway, the first sign of civilization would be scattered little farmhouses. So Clint headed toward the farmhouses. He hoped he could flag down a car quickly and use the driver's cell phone.

As Clint walked, he kept seeing Melina that day in her little blue dress, barefoot, standing in the doorway, her silken black hair blowing around her face. She had looked like an angel. He had loved her as he had not yet loved any girl. How could it all have been a lie? He wondered how he could ever get over this and trust again. Ever.

A car was coming. Clint ran to the middle of the road and began wildly waving his arms for them to stop. The car did not reduce its speed. It swerved around him and sped away. There was a woman at the wheel. Clint didn't blame her for not stopping. Here was a guy in the middle of nowhere, blood streaming down his arms, dirty, strange looking. She was scared, and she had a right to be. She thought it was some wild man who would harm her if she stopped. She would have had to be crazy to stop. But maybe she would report what she had just seen on her cell phone and that would bring the police.

Clint kept on walking. Melina's voice tormented him, her plaintive little voice with the cute accent pleading for help. How could she have lied all those times? Maybe, Clint thought, they were forcing her to be part of this crime. Maybe she was just a kid caught up in something she couldn't control. But Clint did not entertain that possibility for long.

Another car came into view. It was an old sedan moving more slowly. Clint ran to the middle of the highway again, waving his arms desperately. This time the car slowed. There was an old man wearing a baseball cap at the wheel. He stopped, but he didn't roll down the window.

"What's wrong?" he shouted at Clint.

"I've been attacked by criminals," Clint said. "I need to call the police. Do you have a cell phone?"

"Nope. Don't have a cell phone," the old man said. Something about Clint must have reassured him. He rolled down the window and said, "I'll give you a ride to the gas station, son. It's not far from here."

"Thanks," Clint said gratefully, climbing in the passenger side of the car.

The old man looked about 80 years old. Maybe he remembered a time when most people could be trusted, and that's why he was willing to give Clint the benefit of the doubt. Or maybe he was at an age when he was willing to take risks. Either way, Clint was thankful.

"You okay, son? You're bleeding pretty bad," the man said as they pulled into the service station.

"I'm fine. The wounds aren't deep. Thanks a lot, mister," Clint said, climbing from the car and hurrying toward the station.

Clint grabbed the phone and dialed 911. He told them everything. He explained that his house was occupied by criminals who planned to surprise his family as they came home and rob them. Clint told the police that the criminals in his house were the same people who had murdered Edgar Sandusky.

A police car came screaming up to the

gas station five minutes later to pick Clint up.

"We have police officers at your home right now," the officer told Clint.

"Thank God," Clint said. His wrists throbbed with pain and his shirtsleeves were hard with dried blood, but no one could harm his family now. He was so relieved, he felt like weeping.

The police officer asked Clint if he wanted to go to the ER to get his wounds cleaned and bandaged, but Clint refused. He just wanted to go home.

When they pulled up to the Asuna home, there were several police cars parked in the driveway and on the street.

"Did you guys get the woman hiding in the house?" Clint asked. "She was supposed to hold down the fort until the other two got here."

"Wasn't anybody here when we arrived," the police sergeant said.

Clint wondered what happened to Hyma and Melina. Maybe something went wrong with their plans. Maybe Irini saw the police coming and fled. Then she could have warned the others.

When Clint's parents came home, the police talked to the whole family. Clint had told Melina's fake story to the police, about the danger her life was in.

"That's their method of operation," the officer said. "They target jewelers who deal in really good stuff. They find a way to worm their way into the confidence of a member of the family. They use a ruse to make sure there's a safe in the house. Then, when the time is right, they pounce. Sometimes the older woman, Irini, is the bait. She won the confidence of an elderly man in San Francisco, and they got all his dead wife's jewelry, including an heirloom brooch. That's what Edgar Sandusky was investigating. More often they use the girl. She's no poor little rich girl, and she's not 16. She's 19 going on 40. She's an experienced criminal. They apparently killed Edgar Sandusky because he would have blown their scheme to rob your family."

"I feel really stupid," Clint said.

"Don't," the officer said. "They are experts at fooling people. Melina especially. And being so pretty doesn't hurt."

"Do you think you'll be able to catch them?" Clint's dad asked.

"We're sure going to try. It's not robbery anymore. It's murder. They took the life of a good man, a former cop, a friend to many of us," the sergeant said grimly.

The police finished their investigation and left. Clint's mom cleaned and bandaged the cuts on his arms. Clint apologized profusely to his parents for his mistake in judgment. His loving parents understood and forgave him. They were most thankful that their family had not been harmed. They also hoped Clint had learned a valuable lesson from it all.

....

When Clint returned to school the next day, he got a lot of ribbing from his friends. There was no good way to explain how he had been so completely tricked by Melina Barja.

"Talk about doofuses," Ricky said. "Man, you were so goofy over that bad chick that if she'd told you she was from Mars and being followed by gnomes from Neptune you wouldn't have doubted it."

Clint sighed. "I guess I did go a little ape over her . . . she was so sincere and, you know, in need of help . . ."

Clint felt glum and betrayed. He always thought he was a pretty savvy guy, but this had cut the legs right out from under him. From the first moment that little monster had crouched beside his truck crying for help, he was a goner, a poor fish with bait in his mouth.

Over the next few days, Clint learned that Irini and Hyma had been arrested trying to flee to Mexico. They were not from Greece or Italy. They were from Florida. They were American thugs who used foreign accents to serve their purposes. But there was no sign of Melina.

10

ON FRIDAY, as Clint was driving home from school, he spotted something he couldn't believe. Melina was standing by the drugstore, apparently waiting for Clint to drive by. There she was, wearing that little blue dress, her feet in white sandals, her dark hair blowing around her face. She waved to Clint, and he pulled to the curb. Melina came walking to the driver's side of the truck.

"Please," she said, "just let me talk to you for a few minutes, and then you can call the police if you still want to."

Clint realized he was crazy to sit here at the wheel of his truck and listen to a word from the girl's mouth. But he had loved her so much. She had meant so much to him that for his own peace of mind he wanted to hear what she had to say. Maybe, Clint thought, this horrible experience would be easier to live with if there was some semblance of an excuse for her. So Clint let her climb into the cab of the truck, and they drove off to a quiet street. He parked under a spreading Brazilian pepper tree.

"Telling you I'm sorry is not enough," Melina said. "I did a terrible thing to you. You were so kind to me, and I betrayed you. I feel so guilty it is eating me alive."

"I really cared about you," Clint said bitterly and sadly. "I really kind of loved you, Melina, in a way I've never felt about a girl before." Clint shook his head.

"I know it does not excuse me, but Irini and Hyma are my real parents," Melina said. "My family has always been this way. We are criminals. I have never known anything else. I was raised like this. When I was a small child, I stole for them. My parents talked to merchants in stores while I ran around taking things."

"But, Melina, how could you have done this to me? To my family? You could have gotten my parents and my little sister killed. You knew that they had murdered a good man, and you still went along with the scheme," Clint said.

"Hyma killed the detective. Hyma is a cruel, evil man. I am ashamed that he is my blood. But what could I do? He is my father." She reached out and laid her small, soft hand on Clint's arm. "I am sorry with all my heart for everything. Please try to forgive me. It was not only you who fell in love with me. I also fell in love with you, Clint. Hyma was planning to kill you. He said that was the only way to make sure everything went well. I stopped him, Clint. I made him tie you up instead. Clint, do you have it in your heart to forgive me?"

Clint turned and looked at the girl. Disheveled and weary looking, her dark eyes rimmed with tears, she was still the most beautiful girl he had ever seen. Looking at this girl had once given Clint goosebumps. Her shimmering eyes had melted his heart and clouded his judgment so many times.

"I'll try to forgive you, Melina," Clint said.

Melina fell into Clint's arms, the tears pouring down her face. "I cannot go to prison, Clint. They will charge me with the murder too. I would never have killed that man, but they will accuse me too. I will go to prison for many years. Oh, Clint, I will grow old and ugly there. I will be like a caged bird, trapped until it dies . . . " she wept.

"What do you want, Melina?" Clint asked.

"Drive me to Mexico," she said. "Tell the border guards we are husband and wife. I know that once I'm in Mexico I can slip into the countryside. I will start fresh and live a good life. Please Clint, for the love you have felt for me, help me this last time . . . "

Clint started up the truck. "It's about 25 miles to the Mexican border," he said.

"I will write to you, Clint," she said. "And maybe we will yet be together. I'm really innocent. My parents must pay for their crimes, but I am innocent . . . "

Clint turned south, toward Mexico. But then he suddenly turned east. He slowed in front of a large building.

"Clint!" the girl screamed, "Don't stop here!"

Clint reached over and seized her wrist,

holding it in a viselike grip. Then he hit his horn.

"Clint! No! No!" Melina screamed as the police came out of the building.

"This is Melina Barja," Clint told them as they surrounded the truck. "She's wanted for robbery and the murder of Edgar Sandusky. You already have the rest of the gang in custody."

Clint sat at the wheel of the truck as they took the sobbing girl away. Her feet slipped from her sandals as she struggled. The shoes lay there on the sidewalk, askew. The last image Clint had was her body bent over in her little blue dress, her long dark hair tangled, and her feet bare.

Clint drove slowly home. He saw haloes around the streetlights, and he realized he was weeping. Dale and Ricky should see him now, he thought. He would never live it down. But they wouldn't see him. Nobody would. By the time he was home, he would be all right. No, he wouldn't be all right. But nobody would know that he wasn't.

"Good-bye, Melina," Clint said to the night stars. "Good luck. You'll be okay. Even birds in a cage sing sometimes . . . "

A TEST OF YOUR ANIMAL INSTINCTS

1. **Approximately how much food does a full-grown elephant eat per day?**
2. **How does an armadillo get across rivers?**
3. **What bird flies in first-class comfort?**
4. **How does the male African hornbill keep the female in line after mating?**
5. **What determines the gender of alligators?**
6. **How do hornets amuse themselves?**

Answers

1. **400 pounds worth.** In the Bronx Zoo, elephants are fed 300 pounds of hay, 16 quarts of grain, and 16 quarts of carrots, apples, and stale Italian bread.
2. He gulps down air until his stomach is like a balloon, and then he floats across.
3. The albatross, a bird that can doze while he flies.
4. He plasters her up in the hollow of a tree and doesn't release her until the eggs are hatched.
5. The temperature. If the eggs are incubated below 86 degrees Fahrenheit, then females are born; above 93, and the offspring are male.
6. They drink themselves silly, swilling the juices of fermented fruit until they fall into a stupor.

Also by Barbara Seuling:

HOW TO WRITE A CHILDREN'S BOOK AND GET
    IT PUBLISHED

YOU CAN'T SHOW KIDS IN UNDERWEAR AND
    OTHER LITTLE-KNOWN FACTS ABOUT
    TELEVISION

THE LAST COW ON THE WHITE HOUSE LAWN
    AND OTHER LITTLE-KNOWN FACTS ABOUT
    THE PRESIDENCY

YOU CAN'T EAT PEANUTS IN CHURCH AND
    OTHER LITTLE-KNOWN LAWS

YOU CAN'T SNEEZE WITH YOUR EYES OPEN
    AND OTHER FREAKY FACTS ABOUT THE
    HUMAN BODY*

*Coming soon from Ivy Books

ELEPHANTS CAN'T JUMP

& OTHER FREAKY FACTS ABOUT ANIMALS

Barbara Seuling

IVY BOOKS • NEW YORK

Ivy Books
Published by Ballantine Books
Copyright © 1985 by Barbara Seuling

Library of Congress Catalog Card Number: 84-10219

ISBN 0-8041-0351-8

This edition published by arrangement with E.P. Dutton (Lode-
star Books), a division of NAL Penguin, Inc.

Manufactured in the United States of America

First Ballantine Books Edition: October 1988

to Gwenn, my zoo pal, niece,
conspirator, French tutor, and good friend,
with love

Contents

ELEPHANTS CAN'T JUMP

& OTHER FREAKY FACTS ABOUT ANIMALS

1

TOOTH AND NAIL

Physical Characteristics

○ Elephants can't jump. Although they have the same bones in their feet as other animals, theirs are more closely packed, giving them none of the flexibility or spring mechanism that enables others to jump.

○ The shark's skin is covered with denticles, tiny little teeth, which can scrape the skin off a human brushing against them. Some people believe that ancient Roman soldiers wore helmets made of sharkskin.

○ The sperm whale has the largest brain of any mammal. The largest sperm whale brain on record weighs a little more than 17 pounds.

○ The giraffe has the same number of neck bones as a mouse—seven.

○ Shells of giant clams have been used as holy water fonts in European churches. Giant land tortoise shells have been used as bathtubs.

○ Woodpeckers don't get headaches when they hammer continually on hard wood because their skull bones contain many air spaces which act as shock absorbers.

○ The shark doesn't have a bone in its body: Its skeleton is made completely of cartilage. The sea horse has a skeleton, but it's on the outside.

○ The octopus once had a shell, like the snail, the clam, and the oyster. Its tentacles grew as its shell got smaller, and eventually the shell disappeared.

○ For years, it was believed that giraffes made no sound at all. A study was made, and it turns out that the giraffe can, indeed, make sounds as other animals do, but it just doesn't care to. Giraffes prefer body language when talking to other giraffes.

○ The skin of the moloch, an Australian lizard, is like a blotter. If the animal stands in water so that only its feet are submerged, soon its skin is wet all over.

○ The barn owl's face, shaped like a dish, collects sounds like a radar screen.

○ The Komodo dragon, the largest lizard on earth, is 10 feet long and weighs as much as 250 pounds.

○ The lips of a hippopotamus are nearly 2 feet wide.

○ Birds can sing more than one song apiece. The robin and the meadowlark, for example, have about fifty different songs. Some bird couples sing duets, each bird singing different notes. It is almost impossible to tell where one bird leaves off and another begins.

○ The wings of bats are actually membranes of skin connecting long, slender fingers.

○ The kiwi of Australia has only tiny wing sprouts and cannot fly like other birds, but it also has something no other bird has: nostrils at the tip of its beak to help it sniff worms underground.

○ The tuatara lizard of New Zealand has three eyes—two in the usual place, and one on the top of its head. Other vertebrates, long extinct, had a functional third eye, but this is the only living creature in which it now exists.

○ The dugong, a large, gentle marine mammal, sheds tears when it is in trouble or pain. At one time, the animal was captured and tortured to collect its tears, which were then sold as love charms.

○ A species of salamander called the Proteus, or cave newt, is born with tiny eyes which eventually disappear. Its whole life is spent in dark underground caves.

○ The Falabella horse of Argentina, when full grown, is about as big as a German shepherd.

○ Elephant tusks are actually teeth and sometimes grow 11 feet long. The inside molars are as big as bricks. When an elephant has a toothache, he has a big problem. If the root of a tusk is infected, the pain can be so great that the elephant will extract the tooth—or tusk—himself, by wedging it in the crotch of a tree and pulling.

○ Snow fleas, which live 22,000 feet above sea level in the Himalayas, freeze solid each night, when the temperature drops drastically, and thaw out the next day.

○ The koala has an appendix that is 6 to 8 feet long.

○ Moose are so nearsighted that some have mistaken automobiles for their mates.

○ A shark may have twenty-four thousand teeth —all razor sharp—in its lifetime.

○ A beaver must chew wood every day, or its teeth would grow so long it would not be able to eat, and it would starve to death. One beaver chews down hundreds of trees in a year.

○ The yak's milk is pink.

○ Dogs sweat through their foot pads. Cows sweat through their noses. Hippopotamuses sweat all over—in red when they are excited. The color is from an oily secretion that keeps a hippo's hide from drying and cracking.

○ Some animals have rarely been seen alive—the giant squid, for example. Dead specimens show that it can reach a length of 55 feet and has eyes 9 inches across. Longman's beaked whale has never been seen alive. It is known only from two skulls that washed ashore, one in Australia in 1926 and one in East Africa in 1955.

○ Cows give more milk when they listen to music. Some cows show a distinct preference for Mozart.

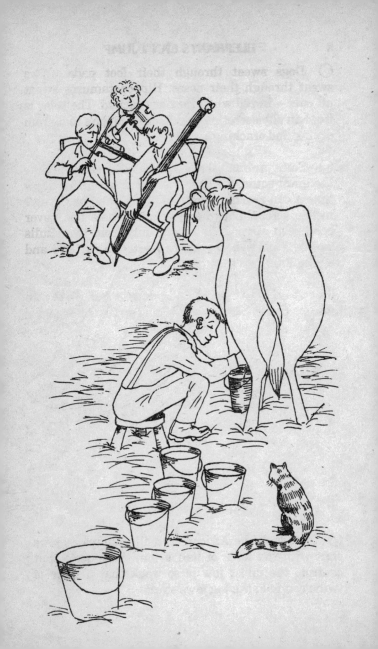

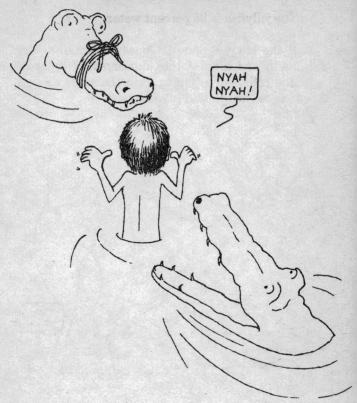

○ Although the African crocodile clamps its jaws shut with the force of half a ton, the muscle that controls the upper jaw is so weak that a piece of twine can hold the big jaws shut.

○ The jellyfish is 95 percent water.

○ If the lowly sponge is squeezed through very fine mesh and divided into thousands of separate bits, the cells will rejoin to form the same sponge, identical to the original in every way.

2

HOME SWEET HOME

Dwellings

○ Inside the Carlsbad Caverns in New Mexico, where millions of bats make their home, each bat hangs in one square inch of space.

○ Tailor ants, found in Australia, Africa, and India, use their own offspring to sew together leaves for their nests. For thread, they use the silken threads secreted by their larvae. For needles, they use the larvae themselves, pushing them in and out of the holes in the leaves.

○ Although the mounds of magnetic termites in Australia may be 20 feet high and solid enough for elephants to use as scratching posts, they are only a few inches across. The skinny sides are exposed to the direct rays of the sun during the hottest part of the day, keeping the mound from overheating. In the morning and late afternoon, the cooler times of the day, the wider sides are exposed. It is a perfect example of a solar home, obtaining the maximum benefit from the sun's rays to keep temperatures inside the mound at a comfortable level.

○ Some hermit crabs have made their homes in soup cans. Having no shells of their own to protect their soft and vulnerable bodies from enemies, they usually "borrow" the cast-off shells of other creatures. When they are young, this is easy, but as they grow, they must move to larger and larger homes, and large shells are hard to find. Some crabs will use anything that can be made into a dwelling, including coconut shells, parts of lamps, plaster models—and soup cans.

○ There is a luminous glowworm found in only one spot on earth—the subterranean depths of New Zealand's Waitomo Caverns. Resembling twinkling stars in the darkness of the caves, the tiny creatures use their lights to lure prey to them.

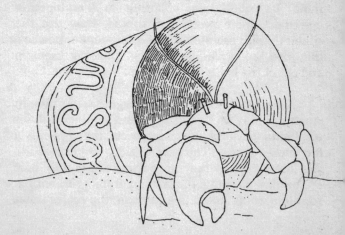

○ Shortly after they are born, barnacles glue themselves to a surface and stay in that one place for life. The substance they use to bond themselves to their permanent address is about twice the strength of epoxy and stronger than any glue manufactured by man.

○ The chipmunk builds his home complete with indoor plumbing. The underground dwelling has a separate chamber off the bedroom that serves as a bathroom and drains into the ground away from the living quarters.

○ Some alligators live in nests that are a thousand years old.

○ Weaverbirds build huge condominiums—communal dwellings like apartment houses—that contain nearly a hundred separate nests.

○ Pupfish have the most restricted home on earth. They live only in one place—the pools on a rock shelf in the Amargosa Desert in Ash Meadows, Nevada.

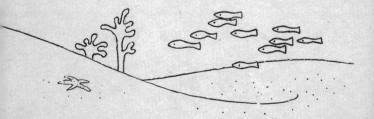

○   The fox squirrel builds its home on the same principle as that for thermal underwear: It is insulated in a manner that makes use of dead-air spaces.

○   Sponges serve as apartment houses for very small sea animals. The sponge's passageways provide many compartments in which the tiny creatures can make their homes.

○   The peregrine falcon, which usually nests in high cliffs and canyons across the United States, has been known to nest on the windowsills of skyscrapers in New York City. The bird finds the windowsills a good substitute when it is away from home.

○   During the day, the oilbird of South America lives deep inside mountain caves where it is totally dark. At dusk, the oilbird flies out only to search for food, then returns to the cave.

○   Bee hives are air-conditioned. In hot weather bees place drops of water or diluted honey around the hive and fan their wings, keeping the hive cool.

○ Mole rats of East Africa live in underground colonies in much the same way that some insects do, conducting their lives in subterranean chambers within a large society headed by a queen.

○ Kirtland's warbler, an endangered bird, depends on forest fires for its survival. Only the intense heat of such a fire can burst open the tight cones of the jack pine tree, dispersing its seeds. These seeds eventually grow into a new forest of young pines, where the bird thrives. When the trees grow too tall, the birds leave.

○ There can be eighty thousand bees living in one hive.

○ The African lovebird, a small parrot, cuts leaves into long strips with its beak, then tucks these strips into its feathers to fly them to its home-building site, where they are used for nesting material.

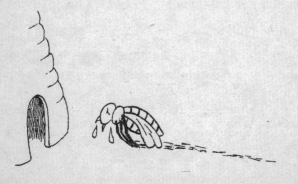

◯ Ross's seal does not live on land or in the water; it lives exclusively on the floating ice of the Ross Sea in the Antarctic.

◯ The bald eagle builds and adds on to a nest until it is about 12 feet deep and 8½ feet wide— about the same size as the average child's room.

◯ Army ants build houses out of their own suspended bodies, each one clinging to another. Within this living structure, a queen is sheltered, and young are born and raised.

◯ The prairie dog's burrow is a 12-foot hole, straight down, into which the animal dives head first.

○ Once beavers decide on a site for their home, they cannot be persuaded to change their minds—not with dynamite, traps, or even floods. The only thing that will make beavers leave their home is lack of food.

3

TASTY TIDBITS

Eating Habits

○ The panda's diet is almost exclusively bamboo, and it can consume about 90 pounds of it a day, which is one reason why pandas are hard to keep in captivity.

○ A full-grown elephant eats about 400 pounds of food a day. In the jungle, this consists of leaves, fruits, grasses, twigs, and bark. At the Bronx Zoo in New York, the elephants are fed 300 pounds of hay, 16 quarts of grain, and 16 quarts of carrots, apples, and stale Italian bread.

○ Some ants become living storage tanks to hold food for the whole colony's use in emergencies. They eat until they grow into such huge balls that they can hardly move. During hard times, they regurgitate the stored food.

○   Termites eat wood. However, without the help of certain microorganisms that live inside them, they would not be able to digest it. They would eat and eat and eat—and still starve to death.

○   Two-headed snakes are occasionally born. The two heads fight over food, even though it will go into the one stomach that they share. When they are really angry, they might try to swallow each other. Normal snakes will sometimes swallow snakes longer than themselves.

○ The pouch under a pelican's bill can hold up to 25 pounds of fish, or 3 gallons of water.

○ The anglerfish has a kind of fishing rod growing out of its head, with a lure at the end to attract its victims.

○ Leopards take their prey up into a tree to eat it. Sometimes, the meal can be a baby giraffe or antelope that is bigger than the leopard itself.

○ Ants have devised many clever ways to secure a food supply. Some keep gardens where they collect bits of leaves to compost for the raising of mushrooms. Some raise herds of aphids, which they milk for their nutritious secretions. Others, more aggressive, make war and raid and loot the seed and grain warehouses of other ant colonies.

○ Wolves and wild dogs are able to swallow food, which fills their bellies but remains undigested, while they are out hunting. When they arrive home, they then disgorge the undigested food to feed their young and those who stayed at home to guard the den.

○ Hedgehogs have been known to steal milk directly from the cow.

○ There are crabs that climb trees to snip off coconuts.

○ To crack open an egg, the Egyptian vulture throws stones at it.

○ Sled dogs can get drunk from eating fresh shark meat, which is toxic.

○ The tiny shrew has such a delicate nervous system and metabolism that, unless it eats every hour or two, it will starve to death.

○ Crows have been seen stealing bait and fish from fishing lines left in holes in the ice in Norway and Sweden. They draw in the lines with their beaks and hold them down with their feet to keep them from slipping back into the water.

○ A heron, wading in the water, will hold a small feather in its beak and watch quietly for a fish to go by. When it spots one, it drops the feather. As the fish goes toward the lure, the heron snatches it.

○ Coyotes in Los Angeles have been known to sneak into the backyards of wealthy homes at night and sip water from the swimming pools.

○ Alligators weed their waterholes constantly, to keep them free of tangled seaweed and water lily stems, so that turtles—the alligators' favorite food —will have a clear place to swim.

○ Unfortunately, the leatherback turtle loves to eat jellyfish. Plastic bags, which look like jellyfish floating on the surface of the water, get swallowed by the huge turtles, causing serious internal distress.

○ Victims of the giant water bug present an eerie spectacle. The beetle paralyzes its victim—a frog, perhaps—then sucks the juices out of its body, so that all that is left looks every bit like the original frog, but is actually only an empty shell which collapses at the slightest touch.

○ Light fish, which live along the Indonesian coral reefs, have built-in searchlights under their eyes, which help them search for food by beaming light through the water. The light is given off by luminescent bacteria that collect in pouches under the fish's eyes.

4

A LITTLE TRAVELING MUSIC, PLEASE

Getting Around

○ Spiny lobsters march in caravan fashion when they migrate, each lobster latching on to the one in front of it. They march so doggedly that when a group of them was removed from the sea and placed in a vinyl pool for an experiment, they kept going around and around, single file, for two weeks.

○ Some South African shrews are so small that they travel through tunnels dug by earthworms.

○ Penguins can't fly, but when they are underwater, they swim as though they were in flight, their flippers and feet propelling them swiftly through the water. Some penguins dive deeper than can people equipped with scuba gear.

27

GETTING OFF AT
THE NEXT STOP,
PLEASE.

○ Tiny snails embed themselves in the mud on
the feet of wading birds. When the birds move, the
snails get a free ride.

○ Camel feet are excellent for walking in sand. Each foot is made up of two big toes that are covered with thick, tough pads and connected by a web of skin. In mud, however, the camel slips and slides and is practically helpless.

○ The hummingbird, sometimes only 2½ inches long, flies 500 miles, without stopping, over the Gulf of Mexico on its migration journey to the Caribbean islands.

○ Sharks must keep moving or they will suffocate. Other fish have air bladders that enable them to breathe even when they are still. Sharks do not have this device, so when they stop moving, water can't flow over their gills to supply them with oxygen, which they need to live.

○ Most rabbits are helpless in water, but one species, the marsh rabbit of the southeastern United States, swims and dives. When it wants to rest, it builds a raft of reeds, climbs aboard, and sails along.

○ Cats have whiskers on the back of their front legs, as well as around their mouths. Their leg whiskers pick up air vibrations and help them get around in the dark.

○ Before monarch butterflies make a long journey, they sunbathe to gather enough heat to warm up their thoracic muscles, which control their wings.

○ Creeping slowly from one branch to another, the sloth rarely comes down out of the trees even for a drink. If it does land on the ground, it has to walk on the sides of its feet, because its toes are permanently curved under into a hooked position. These hooks enable the animal to hang upside down securely, from which position it eats, sleeps, mates, and even gives birth.

○ When birds fly in V formation on their long migration journeys, they help one another to conserve energy. The eddies created around one bird in flight help the bird just behind it. The eddies around that bird, in turn, help the next in line, and so forth. The only one who gets no help is the leader, at the head of the V, so he is replaced often by another bird.

○ Swans, ducks, and some other birds cannot fly during the period in which they are molting.

○ African jacanas, birds also known as lily-trotters, walk across lily pads on their long toes without sinking.

○ The only way a bat can get started in flight is to drop from its sleeping perch into the air. Once it is flying, it cannot stop until it is ready to latch on to another perch.

○ The ostrich can run as fast as a racehorse.

○ Wolves can travel a distance of 30 to 40 miles in a single night.

○ The huge albatross, the world's largest flying creature, with a wingspan of 12 feet, is dependent on the wind for flight. Without a breeze, it cannot move and is trapped on the ocean until a wind strong enough to enable it to lift off comes along.

○   Mudskippers of Australia, Africa, and Asia are fish that live in rivers, but when the rivers dry up, the fish "row" across land until they come to more water. Some even climb trees in their travels.

○   To swim across a river, an armadillo gulps air until its stomach is full, then slides into the water and floats across like a balloon.

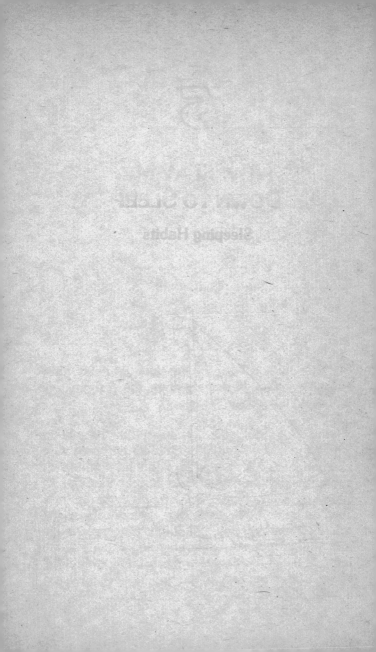

5

NOW I LAY ME DOWN TO SLEEP

Sleeping Habits

○ The huge albatross can sleep while it flies. Helped by the updraft of airwaves, the bird can doze at a speed of 25 miles an hour.

○ The lungfish lives through the dry season in Africa by burrowing down into the mud, curling up in a ball, and sealing itself in with a layer of its own slime. Inside this cozy shelter, it goes to sleep. As the water dries up, the mud hardens around it in a clay coating. When the rainy season comes, the water softens the clay and the fish emerges, alive and well. European explorers used to ship these hard balls of clay home, where they would be dropped in water and, as the clay dissolved, release a live fish.

○ The tuatara lizard of New Zealand sleeps about 90 percent of the time. It is so lethargic that it sometimes falls asleep in the middle of dinner.

○ Although all animals rest sometimes, it is believed that some do not really sleep. Goats, for example, rest about eight hours a day, but they never close their eyes and are constantly alert.

○ Horses, giraffes, and some other four-legged animals sleep standing up, although the giraffe will sometimes lean against a tree. Elephants usually sleep standing up, otherwise they might crush themselves. If they do lie down, they have to rock themselves from side to side to get their big bodies upright again.

○ When a gorilla family goes to bed, they make a nest of branches and leaves in the crotch of a tree. If the male is really heavy, he may be too big for the tree, and he may sleep at the base of it. This led observers to believe that the male gorilla was guarding his family. The family rarely stays in the same place two nights in a row.

○ When sea otters go to sleep at night, they wrap themselves in long strands of kelp, to keep from being separated from their companions. During the night, they may drift miles out to sea, tied together in the seaweed.

○ Many animals hibernate, or sleep through the winter, but none sleep as soundly as the bat. Some have been found coated with ice, yet awaken as good as new when the weather gets warm.

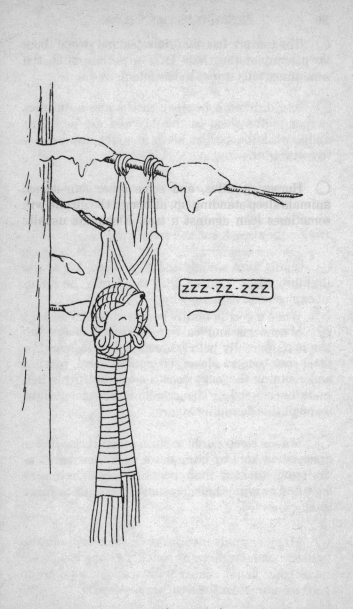

ZZZ·ZZ·ZZZ

○ Birds don't fall off their perches when they sleep because their toes lock in place around the twig or branch on which they sit.

○ One difference between moths and butterflies is that moths sleep in the day and are active at night, while butterflies sleep at night and are active during the day.

○ Parrot fish, which live in undersea coral caves, pull a blanket of mucus, or slime, over themselves when they go to sleep. In the morning, when they awake, they break out and swim away.

○ Quails form a circle and go to sleep, but at the slightest hint of danger, they burst into the air in an explosion of flapping wings.

○ After a good meal, the crocodile naps on the banks of the river with its jaws agape. In hops the little spur-winged plover, or crocodile bird, picking and cleaning the huge beast's teeth, getting a free meal as it works. The crocodile can sleep right through this dental flossing.

○ Wolves sleep outdoors in temperatures 40 degrees below zero by lying down with their backs to the wind, tucking their noses between their rear legs, and burying their faces under their thick furry tails.

6

YOU WERE MEANT FOR ME

Perpetuating the Race

○ After mating, the male African hornbill plasters up his mate in the hollow of a tree or cave. Only a small opening remains, through which he passes food to her. Inside, the brooding female lays her eggs, not breaking out until the eggs are hatched.

○ Male spiders are often eaten by the female immediately after mating, so they have developed devious means to ensure their survival. The male of one species presents the female with a carefully wrapped "wedding" present, usually a fly, and hopes that he will have time to mate with her and escape with his life before she finishes unwrapping his gift.

○ Certain fish off the California coast come onto the beaches once each year during high tide, riding the waves in to shore by the thousands, to lay their eggs in the sand. These fish, called grunions, spawn in holes drilled by the females, and ride back out to sea on the next huge wave, leaving the eggs to develop in the sand and be carried back out to sea when they are about to hatch.

○ Male bowerbirds of Australia and New Guinea construct elaborate courting palaces to which they lure females in order to mate. The bowers are carefully constructed, sometimes big enough for a human to enter, and are decorated with brightly colored or glittering objects—bits of colored glass, beetle wings, bleached bones, feathers, berries, and plastic toys. Fresh flowers are also used, and are replaced when they begin to wilt. Some birds even paint their walls with paintbrushes made from twigs stripped of bark, dipped in a mixture of saliva and charcoal or berry juice.

○ The swordtail fish of Mexico changes sex in the middle of its life. While it is female, it has babies. When it becomes a male, it fertilizes eggs.

○ Most male seals and sea lions are bachelors. In a herd, only about 4 percent of the males mate with the females and produce offspring, fighting off all those smaller and weaker males who compete with them.

○ Some animals have been crossed with each other successfully. A lion and a tiger, for example, produced a liger; a leopard and a jaguar have produced a jagulep; and a zebra and a donkey—a zeedonk. Usually the offspring of such crosses are

sterile, otherwise zoos would be filled with such creatures as ligerjaguleps.

○ Female sea horses lay their eggs directly into the male's pouch, and he carries them around until they hatch.

○ The mayfly has only two hours to spend on this earth, and uses them for just one purpose—mating. It does not even have a working mouth, because it doesn't need one: It has no time to eat.

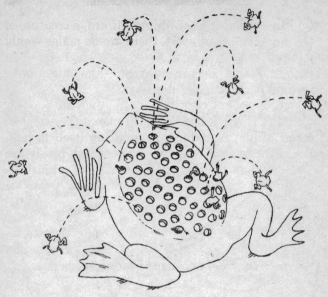

○ The Surinam toad spreads fertilized eggs over the female's back. The eggs settle into little pockets in her skin where they develop and hatch, at which point tiny little toads seem to burst out of their mother's back.

○ Right after he hatches, the male anglerfish grabs onto his sister with his teeth and hangs on for dear life, until the skin of the female actually grows around him, and he becomes a part of her. As the female grows, the male remains a small appendage growing out of her skin, becoming useful only when he is needed to fertilize her eggs.

○ In some species of whiptail lizard, a creature of
the American Southwest, there are no males—only
females. They give birth to females—by means of a
process called parthenogenesis—and these give
birth to more females, and so on.

○ The single-celled amoeba, among the simplest
forms of life, reproduces by splitting itself in half.
For some reason, the two halves that result are
younger than the original "parent"; these must develop and mature before they are able to divide
again.

○ Computers are being used to bring animals together for "dates." This system may be the only
means of survival for some endangered species.

7

IN THE NURSERY

Baby Care

○ A crocodile's first bath takes place in its mother's jaws. The mother crocodile watches her nest deep in the sand, for signs that her eggs are ready to hatch. When the babies appear, she takes them in her teeth, marches down to the water, and swishes them around in her mouth to wash off all the sand.

○ When they are a little older, baby crocodiles thrash around in the water doing the dog paddle to stay afloat. Only after they swallow some stones, which are used for digestion, do they gain the proper balance to swim horizontally.

○ The embryos of sand tiger sharks fight one another in the womb until only one is left at the time of birth.

⭕ Armadillo mothers almost always have four babies at a time, all the same sex, and identical in every way, down to the exact number of hairs on their undersides.

◯ Some baby birds have a strong instinct to follow the first moving thing they see after they are born, as though it were their mother. Ducks in Bali have followed a flag stuck on a pole and have stayed within sight of it while they grazed in the rice fields.

◯ When an alligator's eggs are incubated below 86 degrees Fahrenheit, all females are born. If the temperature is above 93 degrees, the offspring are male. This oddity may be a clue to why dinosaurs became extinct. A severe climate change could have resulted in several generations of one type of offspring, permitting no procreation and eventually killing off the species.

◯ The cuckoo doesn't build its own nest. Instead, it leaves its eggs in another bird's nest, sometimes tossing out eggs that are already there. The foster mother cares for the orphans, although they may be twice her size. If the cuckoo parent does not get rid of the competition, the hatchlings do the job, nudging their stepbrothers and stepsisters to the edge of the nest and pushing them out.

◯ Megapodes, big thick-legged birds of Australia and the South Pacific, lay their eggs on a heap of rotting vegetation. The heat from the mass incubates and hatches the eggs. With their responsibilities behind them, the parent birds take off, never returning. Fortunately, the young are born ready to take care of themselves. A minute after hatching, a young bird can fly.

○ The female porcupine is not injured by its baby's quills when giving birth because, for the first few moments of life, the newborn porcupine's quills are soft.

○ A baby blue whale starts out at about 4,000 pounds and gains an additional 200 pounds a day until it reaches its full growth, which is about 150 tons, or 300,000 pounds.

○ Baby giraffes drop several feet to the ground when they are born.

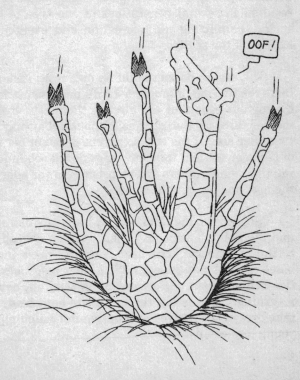

OOF!

○ One species of bee manufactures tiny bags out of polyester materials with "zip" seals at the top, in which it keeps its larvae safe and dry.

○ Koala babies ride around in backseats, because their mothers' pouches are on backward. The tiny embryo crawls from the mother's womb when it is only thirty-two or thirty-three days old, heading up toward the rear pouch, where it fastens on a teat.

○ Some female animals, including bears, weasels, and seals, carry a spare embryo; if something happens to one baby, the spare develops to take its place.

○ Although the codfish lays about 4 million eggs a year, only one will probably survive to become an adult fish. The ling fish lays about 30 million eggs, and only two may survive.

○ A kangaroo mother almost always has babies of different ages and has two different supplies of milk. One nipple supplies one formula of milk for the brand-new baby, while another supplies a diluted solution for the older youngster.

○ When baby ostriches are frightened, they squat and flatten themselves out as much as possible, so that they barely cast a shadow.

○ Although they spend most of their lives in the water, sea lions do not swim naturally. Mothers have to teach their babies the fine points of swimming.

○   A baby whale nudges its mother when it is hungry and places its mouth near the slit where the teat is. The teat comes out, and a large squirt of milk is ejected into the calf's mouth.

○   All baby birds are born with a single tooth which helps them peck their way out of their shells. After the big breakout, the egg tooth disappears.

○ Moose mothers sometimes carry their 70-pound babies on their backs to cross wide expanses of water. Elephant mothers have used their tusks as forklifts to carry their babies across rivers.

○ The platypus is, scientifically speaking, a mammal, yet its mammary glands are undeveloped, and it has no nipples. A baby has to nudge its mother into secreting a milky substance, which it then licks off the mother's stomach.

○ The American opossum gives birth to about twenty babies at a time, each the size of a honeybee. Only thirteen can survive, however, because that is the number of nipples on the mother. So there is a kind of race at birth to reach the nipples, and the first thirteen are the winners.

○ When the mother lion goes off to hunt, a baby-sitter—another female—may stay with the cubs. For her pay, she gets a free meal from the mother's catch.

○ A male mouthbreeder fish acts as a sort of garage for as many as four hundred of his offspring at a time, protecting them from harm. If one tiny stranger gets in with the brood, the father spits it out without losing any of his own.

○ The bitterling fish and the mussel, a mollusk, have one of the most peculiar relationships going. The fish lays her eggs inside the mussel's shell, where they hatch. The fry leave their foster home as soon as they can manage on their own. Clamped on to the baby fish, for a ride out to sea, are the offspring of the mussel.

○ The male and female Emperor penguins take turns caring for their egg, which is laid on solid ice. Then the female goes off, while the male rests the egg on top of his feet and keeps it warm with a fold of his belly skin. After two months, the female comes to take her turn, and the male, thin and hungry because he hasn't eaten a thing in all that time, leaves to eat.

8

CAMOUFLAGE AND OTHER NEAT TRICKS

Survival Tactics

○ The horned toad, a lizard of the Southwest and Mexico, shoots a stream of blood from its eyes when it is upset.

○ When threatened, the bombadier beetle blasts its victim with a small explosion of stinging chemicals.

○ A porcupine, with twenty-five thousand sharp quills, each one equipped with one thousand tiny barbs, has few enemies. The fisher, a large weasel, has learned to flip over the porcupine before the porcupine has a chance to shoot its quills.

○ The electric eel, found in rivers of South America, can send off an electric charge of 600 volts, enough to electrocute a man. Some eels are totally blind from eye damage caused by the electrical charges given off by their fellow eels.

○ The spray of skunks that is so repulsive to humans is used among skunks as a perfume to attract mates.

○ Spiders weave signs of warning into their webs to keep birds and large insects from flying into and damaging their webs.

○ Many lizards, when grabbed by the tail, let their tails snap off and make a fast getaway. A new tail later grows in, but without a bone structure to support it. Until the tail is back to its original size, the lizard suffers a kind of social disgrace and loses its former status in the lizard community.

○ The assassin bug is a master of disguise. It hides behind the carcasses of its dead enemies, termites, to get nearer to the live termites. When one comes to help cart away the dead body, the assassin bug jumps out and attacks it.

○ The sound of wolves howling is often the howl of a single wolf. The sound is composed of different harmonics—to give the impression that there are more animals than there actually are.

○ At the approach of danger, termite guards warn their colleagues by shaking their abdomens against the tunnel walls. The vibrations are picked up and sent further along, and so on, until all members of the colony have received the alert.

○ The queen bee is the only one in the hive with a reusable stinger. Female worker bees lose their stingers in the flesh of their victims, after which they die. Male bees have no stingers at all. The queen, who uses her stinger mainly to kill off rival queens, can retract her stinger without harm.

○ Parent birds remove all traces of eggshell from their nests after their young are hatched, since the light color of the shell lining can attract predators.

◯ The snowshoe rabbit turns from brown to snowy white in the wintertime, making it practically invisible in the snow.

○   The spider crab is a neat dresser. He cuts off pieces of live sponges and wears them on his back. The sponge pieces grow around him to fit. Since sponges taste awful, most animals leave them alone, so the spider crab, in his dandy new suit of clothes, is protected.

○   According to some experts, dolphins send bubbles to the surface to relay messages—perhaps warnings—to other dolphins. They also emit clicks, but no one has figured out exactly what they mean.

○   The Australian sea dragon, a type of sea horse, has leafy-looking extensions growing out of its body that look just like the vines and leaves of real seaweed. Its only defense is to hide itself from enemies with these parts of its own body.

9

HERE I COME,
READY OR NOT

Antics and Amusements

○ Deer play a game of tag in which the one who is "it" tags the other with its hooves.

○ Otters play shoot-the-chutes, a water-slide game. In winter, they take a few quick short steps, then push off for a long slide across the ice.

○ In the 1950s, a playful dolphin moved in close to the bathers at a New Zealand resort and played actively with the youngsters, even allowing a thirteen-year-old girl to climb on its back and go for rides, holding on to its dorsal fin. Historians report that the same thing happened in the ancient Carthaginian seaside resort of Hippo, on the coast of what is now Tunisia, but the dolphin was such a crowd gatherer that it was shooed away to regain privacy for the bathers.

○   Badgers play leapfrog and turn somersaults on the grass.

○   Spotted skunks do handstands, but that's usually a signal that they are about to spray.

○   Fish have been known to play jokes. For example, some have squirted water at attendants in aquariums.

○ Cubs of the North American gray wolf are encouraged to play when they are young, and adult wolves even dig out playgrounds near the den for the pups, enlarging them as the pups grow. The art of playing doesn't die down when they grow older. Adult wolves are known to play tag, run and chase each other, romp with cubs, scare each other by jumping out of hiding places, and play with sticks and bones.

○ When playing, bears like to tumble down hills head over heels.

○ The lyrebird of Australia mimics just about anything it hears. It can copy the sound of a factory whistle, a timber mill saw, the neighing of a horse, and an automobile horn.

○ Hornets love to get drunk. If they can find fermenting fruit, they drink the intoxicating juices until they fall into a stupor, then wake up and start partying again.

○ Crows have a sense of humor and seem to have a great old time playing pranks. One of their favorite games is sneaking up on a sleeping rabbit or cow and making a racket to wake them.

○ Penguins toboggan across the ice on their stomachs.

○ Sea otter mothers float on their backs in the water as they play with their babies, lifting them into the air, fondling and kissing them.

○ Male porcupines will sometimes wrestle for fun, but in order for one to grab the other, they have to be very careful to always face each other. The only place they don't have sharp quills is on their soft bellies.

○ Adult squirrels are very playful, turning somersaults, zipping around in games of chase, rolling in leaves, climbing to the ends of thin, bouncy branches, and swaying playfully in the breeze. They have even been known to use pinecones and paper balls in their games.

10

YOU SCRATCH MY BACK, I'LL SCRATCH YOURS

Peculiar Relationships

◯ Snakes have helped scientists in the study of human diseases and cures. Cobra venom has been found useful in medicine for the relief of severe abdominal pain caused by cancer. The venom of Russell's vipers has been used in the control of hemophilia. Rattlesnake venom is being studied for use in controlling epilepsy.

◯ Seals have been trained by the Navy to work with submarine rockets and mines for undersea war operations.

◯ Poodles were first clipped to make it easier for them to swim. They were brought along by hunters to retrieve birds that were shot down.

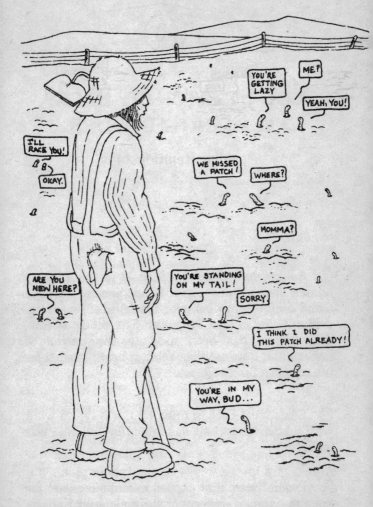

○ Earthworms are a farmer's delight. In one year, the earthworms in an acre of soil can turn over about 18 tons of dirt.

○ A major missile corporation switched from messengers on motorcycles to carrier pigeons to deliver material to its research facility 25 miles away. The pigeons took half the time for a trip and cost a great deal less. Birdfeed for a whole year cost the same as a single day's motorcycle bill.

○ The Aztec Indians of Mexico used little dogs, a tiny Mexican hairless breed, as hot water bottles to warm their feet.

○ Leeches, blood-sucking insects found in the rivers of Africa, were used by European physicians in the Middle Ages to cure all kinds of ailments. For a fever, a band of leeches was placed around the head, where they fastened themselves in place. For indigestion, twenty or thirty were placed on the stomach. In more modern applications, leeches have been used by boxers to drain black eyes, and on patients after plastic surgery.

○   International treaties have been made over the use of guano—bird droppings—which is the richest fertilizer on earth. The largest deposit is off the coast of Peru.

○   Robot designers are studying the spider to design the perfect robotic device. Eight spiderlike legs could alight and walk on almost any uneven surface, an important feature in exploring other planets.

○   A rare kind of silk comes from the *pinnamarina*, or giant silk-bearded clam, found in the Mediterranean Sea. Its milky secretions, in long strands, were once spun into fine cloth and traded in Spain, Italy, and North Africa.

○   New York City has a horse's rights bill. It prohibits working horses in temperatures of 90 degrees or more, and demands that they have a "coffee break"—fifteen minutes' rest for every two hours of work.

○   During the invasion of Normandy in France in 1944, army jeep drivers were helped out in blackouts by glowworms living along the sides of the roads. The tiny lights of these creatures, flashing to attract mates, kept the drivers on the roads.

○   A hand puppet resembling a California condor mother was used to hand-feed a condor chick at the San Diego Zoo. The zoo, dedicated to helping the endangered birds, has a large breeding facility known as the Condorminium.

○ In a pinch, crickets can substitute for thermometers. Add forty to the number of chirps a cricket makes in fourteen seconds, and the result is the temperature, Fahrenheit, within about 2 degrees.

○ The chickens we eat today in the United States are descendants of chickens brought here by Christopher Columbus.

11

ONCE UPON A TIME

Legends and Myths

○ In the Middle Ages, stories abounded in many European countries about werewolves—creatures that were part wolf and part man—who would attack and devour humans. The Danes, for example, believed that if a man's eyebrows met, he would become a werewolf. French and German tradition held that a child born with teeth or in some strange manner, such as feet first, would grow up to be one. People believed to be werewolves were sometimes killed.

○ The ancient Egyptians worshiped cats, and a person could be executed for killing one. In 525 B.C. when the Persian King Cambyses II attacked the Egyptian city of Memphis, he flung cats over the walls of the city. The people inside were so horrified and frightened by this bold act that they surrendered immediately.

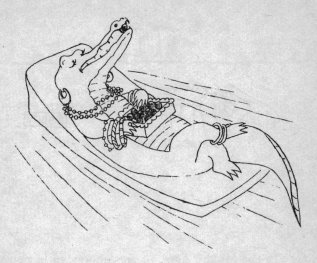

○ Crocodiles, too, were worshiped by the ancient Egyptians, and kept in temple pools, adorned with gold earrings and jeweled bracelets. Sometimes, if a slave was uncooperative, he was tossed into the pool.

RIBBIT!

○ Violinists once handled toads before a concert in the belief that the secretions of the animal would keep their hands from perspiring.

○ When the only surviving ship from Magellan's fleet returned from its historic voyage around the world in 1522, there were some unusual birdskins aboard that created quite a stir. The birds had gorgeous feathers but appeared to have had no bones —or feet. Stories spread about the amazing "bird of God," so special that it stayed aloft forever, with no need for feet on which to rest. The legend remained intact for more than 200 years, even appearing in a work on natural history by Linnaeus in 1735, where it was given the scientific name of *apoda*, which means "footless." Only after many years was it discovered that skillful natives of the East Indies had skinned, drawn, smoked, and prepared actual birds, never before seen by Europeans, to look footless and boneless. These birds today are still known by the name given them at that time—birds of paradise.

○ Manatees, or sea cows, were responsible for tales of mermaid sightings. These large marine mammals, seen at a distance bobbing upright in the water while holding their babies between their flippers, must have looked quite human to sailors who had been at sea for a very long time. Legends grew about mermaids, mysterious sea creatures, half-human, half-fish. Christopher Columbus, probably sighting manatees, reported in his journal that he saw three mermaids, but they were not as beautiful as they had been painted.

○ For centuries, powdered rhinoceros horn has been used in some cultures in the belief that it has magical properties. As a result, certain species of rhinoceros are nearly extinct.

○ The lively dance, the tarantella, was created as an antidote for the bite of a spider. In medieval Italy, people believed that if a person were bitten by a tarantula, or wolf spider, the frantic dancing would rid the victim's body of the spider's poison. Actually that European spider, a very distant cousin of the American tarantula, is harmless.

○   One of the two teeth of the male narwhal whale protrudes from its jaw in an 8-foot spiral. In the Middle Ages, travelers brought many of these teeth home, claiming that they were unicorn horns with magical powers. Many wealthy and powerful people, always wary of assassins, used the tooth to decorate the rims of their drinking cups, in the belief that the "unicorn" magic would counteract any poison that had been dropped into their drinks.

○   The stork is considered good luck to many Europeans, and some people even build nests in their chimneys to attract the birds as they return from their long migration journey.

INDEX

About the Author

BARBARA SEULING is the author-illustrator of many freaky fact books. She says, "This book evolved from the series of freaky fact books, but my interest in animals precedes the series."

Ms. Seuling spends part of her time in Vermont and lives most of the year in New York City with her dog Kaspar—"who is TV material, but we don't want to spoil him with a show biz career."